HOW TO BE A TICKLE SLAVE

First Edition

Published by The Nazca Plains Corporation
Las Vegas, Nevada
2010

ISBN: 978-1-935509-83-7

Published by
The Nazca Plains Corporation ®
4640 Paradise Rd, Suite 141
Las Vegas NV 89109-8000

PUBLISHER'S NOTE
How To Be a Tickle Slave is a work of fiction created wholly by
James T. Medak's imagination. All characters are fictional and any
resemblance to any persons living or deceased is purely by accident.
No portion of this book reflects any real person or events.

Cover Photos
Laurent Hamels and Sandor Kacso

Art Director
Blake Stephens

DEDICATION

Dedicated to Troy Hudson:
it wouldn't have been possible without you.

HOW TO BE A TICKLE SLAVE

First Edition

James T. Medak

CONTENTS

INTRODUCTION

When you get right down to it, tickling is damn sexy.

Think about it: through the very act of wiggling one's fingers into someone else's side, you can reduce them to rubble; to incoherent, babbling shadows of their former selves, helpless to the electric signals you are forcing into their writhing bodies. It is the supreme leveler. The effect is instantaneous, the results are writ-large, it leaves absolutely no kinds of markings or scarings at all, and – let's be honest – it's just hella-fun to watch.

So what, then, is so appealing about seeing a *guy* get tickled? For many (myself included), nothing really beats the sight of a masculine fella crumble via tickle torture. It's like you're watching the dismantling of every single machismo cliché instantaneously, watching tough guys turn into begging machines just because you're dragging a toothbrush across the soles of their feet. Tickling actually *forces* out smiles and laughter, frequently against the victim's will, and most guys – no matter where they hail from – just can't take it. They're helpless just like the rest of us, and, in short, nothing's sexier than a bruised male ego.

When I was a teenage lad in the process of realizing I had both a male foot fetish *and* a strong tickle fetish to go with it, one of the things that guided me through these discoveries was the amount of tickle-fiction available on websites like RopeJock. Guys being put in inescapable bondage positions, ticklish revenge extracted out of them slowly and skillfully, all resulting in the maximum amount of horny punishment that could be inflicted on them – it all blew my mind back in the day. Each new erotic tale challenged what I knew and forced me to think about my fetish in a brand new light. I got obsessed, and delightfully so. One user's website, some years later, said quite simply that "ticklish boys, no matter where they are, need to be tickled" – and I couldn't agree more with that sentiment.

Yet as the years went on (and the internet became more and more open to any takers), it got harder and harder to find those carefully-crafted tickle epics that were so important towards my own psychological development. New writers would try stories all the time – as well they should – but a lack of proper grammar (lolz!) and proper character development lead these stories to be shallow and fleeting, said stories frequently being based around the writer's faint idea of how the tickling of a particular celebrity would be like. During one delightfully intoxicated evening, I had the fool-hardy (and totally pompous) notion to give it a go myself, to write the kind of story that inspired me back in the day – and here I sit, years later, writing an introduction to own naughty little tome…

In short, the best fiction – erotic or otherwise – has to be character-driven, because if you don't care about the people involved, then you don't really care what happens to them either. If you get emotionally invested in their wants and desires, however, then suddenly you are drawn into their world, you *care* about what sort of devious adventures await them, and – most critically – the hot scenarios they are put in just get that much hotter. Something has to be at stake for these things to work (because tickling just for the sake of tickling isn't as interesting as when there's something – a bet, a hidden secret, a personal revelation – that's riding on the outcome). And, above all, you got to try new things. People have written about the fantastic art of foot-licking for years, so finding a new spin on it is nothing short of a challenge – but challenges like this are what makes writing fiction so much fun: sometimes you surprise even yourself with what you come up with.

So, here it is. My collected fictions. Dirty little tales that are frequently culled from my own personal experiences (some of the names even being of real-life people that I wouldn't mind worshipping/tickling more than a few times over). Have a blast reading 'em... 'cos I had hell of a time writing them.

Ticklishly yours,

James T. Medak

FOOT CLUB

The first story I ever wrote. Oh sure, I dabbled in the realms of erotic fiction here and there, but this was the first time that I had actually sat down and wrote something of substance. The writing process on this was purely impulsive: I was very (very) intoxicated and supremely horny at the time, and decided to get all these devious little thoughts down on paper. The next morning, I went over what I had written (making several grammatical adjustments along the way), and I realized I had something here: just a hot little scenario that had been jogging around my head for the past month or so. As with most of my fantasies, it was set at a college campus (hell, anytime I can get a guy in jeans and flip-flops, I'll do it), and things just sort of evolved naturally. It was the response to this that encouraged me to continue on after this, so, welcome to Ground Zero...

And Todd was found out, his greatest weakness suddenly exposed at the moment he least expected it, realizing now that he would be a perpetual footslave to the person who he thought would least control him... and there was nothing he could do about it.

1.

"What the fuck is 'Foot Club'?"

"Dude, just drop it, OK!" sneered Zach, the skater punk that sat in front of Todd every day during his Philosophy of Art class. Todd looked pleading with his blazed blue eyes and collegiate-handsome good looks, but Zach wasn't going to budge. When Zach left to use the restroom in a class two days prior, Todd managed to sneak a peak into Zach's planner during a planned writing exercise. It said that next Tuesday would be a meeting of 'Foot Club'. Todd was a bit intrigued to say the least, and the very fact that Todd even mentioned it to Zach was obviously breaking some sort of protocol – yet that only intrigued Todd more.

Admittedly, Todd didn't care much about forming a friendship with Zach – afterall, the dude wore skater shoes – but Todd couldn't help but be a bit fascinated by what was transpiring. When Todd was a teenager, he began developing his strong, powerful male foot fetish, which started during a Scout camping trip in which he lost a bet, was hog-tied in his tent, and forced to smell and worship the feet of the senior Scouts (aka the ones nearing Eagle). It was a one-time, isolated event designed to humiliate the newest members of the Troop, but its effect still had a powerful effect on the young Todd. He started out seeking revenge – wanting to do the same thing to his captors that they did to him – but soon his desire to get back at the senior Scouts turned into an all-out obsession with men's feet.

It was kind of weird for Todd, as he still liked girls and wound up (surprisingly) being quite the ladies man during his senior year of high school – but when you came right down to it, Todd got turned on the most by guys feet and the very thought of worshipping, tickling, and massaging them. Guys in flip-flops were his favorite, and even though he had a few discreet, intoxicated experiences with some "foot guinea pigs" during his freshmen year in college, the idea of sex with a guy just didn't do anything for Todd. He just wanted feet – it became somewhat of an insular sexual conquest for him, and one that he wasn't able to satisfy for months on end. He had an "understanding" with one of the gay guys on campus, who kindly let Todd worship his feet for hours on end, but as soon as actual emotions were beginning to emerge between them, Todd cut it off – he just wanted foot action with no strings attached (which – incidentally – proved to be a very, very hard thing to get). It was a weird, complicated experience that wound up polarizing his friends around him, but Todd knew he couldn't change who he was: it was better to accept who he was than to fight what he was always secretly thinking about.

Even now, watching as Zach glanced over his shoulder at him every few minutes just to scold him, Todd began wondering what this "foot club" experience was. Oh yeah, he got the reference: *Fight Club* and all that. Hell, he didn't even think it was that tacky of a name. He just wondered what if there were guys around here that shared his fetish? He had a crush on every perpetually sandal-clad frat boy that walked by him, unsure of whether he wanted to dominate them or be dominated by them. Every once in awhile some guy would catch him staring at their bared feet, but Todd was never sure if the glance he got in return was a look of disgust or a wink of acknowledgement. Either way, Todd's feet – in flip-flops and blue jeans for every day the temperature was over 50 – were exactly the kind to get those kinds of glances: size 12 monsters with absolutely perfectly rounded toes. He just got a Feet.TV profile the other week, and already he had made some 30-odd friends, including eight right here in this very state! As turned on as he got by others podiacal treasures, it was kind of surprising how turned on Todd was getting by exhibiting his own soles…

The sharp buzz of the between-classes bell snapped Todd back into reality, and he seemed dazed, just having woken up after dreaming of feet. The small hard-on in his pants simply disappeared the second that Todd saw what was scrawled on the blackboard: "THREE PAGE ESSAY DUE TOMORROW!" That was the most terrifying thing of all, as Todd had *no* idea what the prof was referring to.

As he wandered across the spring-licked campus, nodding at friends and classmates, Todd gradually came to a decision: tomorrow night, he would follow Zach to "Foot Club."

———————

2.

By the time that Tuesday had rolled around, Todd had gotten nervous. He was thinking of nothing but possible worship opportunities, often fantasizing about being tied up on the floor of a fraternity basement, sandaled and barefooted fratboys tickling, poking, prodding, and teasing him, all filming it and putting it up on YouTube in an act of great humiliation. In truth, Todd didn't know why being subjugated to such degradation was appealing to him, but for the time being, that fantasy was all he could think about.

Todd was still reading an incredible new TKLFrat story at 2AM, losing track of time while trapped in a horny state of mind, jacking himself off in nothing but his computer screen glow... at least until his roommate burst in. "Still up?" said the bearded, handsome Doug, as Todd quickly Alt-Tabbed his screen and covered up his massive hardon as non-chalantly as possible. "Oh yeah... you know how Googling yourself can lead you to weird places on the internet." "Ha ha, yeah" sighed Doug in agreement.

Todd hated Doug: not because of who he was (he actually was a well-tempered guy who never got agitated by any of Todd's habits regarding hanging clothes up), but because of what he wore. That's right, Doug wore Chuck Taylors every day. Ever. In his life. He was somewhat of an overachiever and a drama nerd to boot, so between the early classes and late rehearsals, Todd was usually in bed during anytime that his buddy would be unshod. The few glimpses of Doug's foot flesh that he saw were too much for him – he had an unbelievable crush on Doug's feet (and to a lesser extent, Doug), so seeing them as infrequently as he did just drove him up the wall. He and Doug chatted for awhile, but before long they both had turned the lights off and went to bed. Todd, awash with fetish fantasias, wouldn't fall asleep for another three hours.

When he woke up the next day, it was 1PM. He didn't know how he did it, but here was, awake and having just missed three of his classes. Well, fuck. Tonight was Foot Club – he could give himself the day off. After grabbing some cereal, he waded around in his dorm room trying to kill time, popping in some *Doctor Who* but then regretting it 'cos he forgot the Season Two opener had David Tennant barefoot for half the episode, further propelling his fantasies. He tried to do some Spanish homework, but still couldn't get his mind off the topic at hand. Time inched by, but by 5PM, he was saddling up to do some Zach stalking. As he was putting on his hoodie (yes, even with jeans and flip-flops still), Doug walked in.

"Hey man… where you off to?"

Todd remained coy: "I don't know, I just need to go out. Some nights you just need an adventure, you know?" Doug laughed, "Yeah, I know that feeling. Well best of luck." Doug went to his computer and was reaching for a beer in his under-the-counter fridge right as Todd was closing the door.

This was going to be interesting no matter what happened. After getting out of the cafeteria before 6PM (aka before "the rush"), Todd wound up walking near some of the dorm apartments before he found Zach kicking around in the parking lot of the science building. He was with some skater buds, and Todd sat next to a tree in a distance, just waiting for the guys to finish up. Yet they kept skating and skating, and Todd went from sitting to slumping, from slumping to sleeping. When he woke up, he had no sight of Zach nearby. He glanced at his cell – it was 9:43PM. Shit. He then heard what he thought was Zach's voice echoing between the apartments down the road. He clenched his toes together around the sandal thongs and began running as fast as he could in Zach's direction.

When he finally got Zach in sight, he was down to only one other friend who Todd couldn't recognize – all he could tell was that Zach's friend was in flip-flops, and that's all Todd needed. He began walking slowly and less conspicuously behind them, the now-present moonlight helping on the visibility front. After a minute's walking, Zach was soon entering through the ground-level door of a frat house. Todd looked around – no one was watching. After about 30 seconds, he entered the same door, unsure of exactly what building he was entering (Todd never went to many frat parties) or what was to be expected inside. Either way, his heart was beating a lot faster than it normally did.

He heard some noise coming from the basement, and began heading down the creaky frat-house stairs. He was walking one flight down… and there was a second? Man, this was a deep basement. Yet there was a room down there of what looked like… hard concrete… but covered by sand? In this room, there were wooden support pillars scattered around, and in the middle of the sand-accented floor, there was a bunch of barechested guys, forming a circle around a single swinging lightbulb. Todd looked right next to the base of the stairs: a series of discarded A&F t-shirts, hoodies, jackets, and shoes. Yet his inquisitive eye jumped right for the signs, and there were no sandals to be found. None of the guys in the circle had noticed him, so Todd quietly removed his hoodie and undershirt, and walked calmly in his leather sandals towards where the guys were gathered. Much to his surprise…

…they were just talking. Looking at the abs of his fellow peers, he found more six-packs than the Stop-N-Go convenience mart. All these guys… looked good! And were barefoot! There were still quite a few guys in flip-flops, so Todd just assumed that as long as your feet were exposed, you were OK. Todd caught bits of conversations about classes, girls, the kegger this Friday, etc. He was mainly just intrigued by the number of guys around him, all drawn by some strange homoerotic impulse. Oddly, Todd felt safe around here, but he wasn't sure why.

"LISTEN UP!!"

The voice came from Gregg, the tall, dark-haired kid who always wore a suit to his classes. Now, he was down to nothing but his jet-black dress pants, but never had he looked more commanding. The conversations quickly died like ambers in a fire – all eyes were fixed on the half-nude Gregg. "OK, ladies. Good turn out tonight, I must say. But I'm somewhat disappointed, as this means a lot of your are violating the first two rules of Foot Club." That last sentence came out sternly, and the gravity of it had an obvious impact on all. "So let's review," started Gregg. "The first rule of Foot Club is… you do not talk about Foot Club." Just like the movie, Todd thought. "The second rule of Foot Club is… YOU DO NOT TALK ABOUT FOOT CLUB – unless you WANT to get punished. The third rule of Foot Club is that if someone is begging for mercy, you stop. The fourth rule: only two guys to a match. The fifth rule: one match at a time. The sixth rule of Foot Club is… no shirts, and no shoes." The guys let out a holler to this one.

"The seventh rule," Gregg continued, "is that a match must go on as long as it needs to. And the eight rule is… if this is your first night at Foot Club… you HAVE to take part in a match. With that said… who here is at their first Foot Club?" Todd was tempted to raise his hand, but was too timid. He was standing behind a row of guys, so perhaps he could just quietly slip out and get back to –

"I KNOW SOMEONE!"

Todd perked up – it was Zach's voice. "Todd is here!" All the guys turned in the direction of Zach's finger, pointing directly at the flip-flopped Todd, his toes flinching at the sudden attention. "All right!" shouted Gregg. "Zach, since you pointed out the newbie, you gotta match him. Todd! Get over here!"

Todd was frozen. He couldn't move. He couldn't bring himself to do anything, but the group of guys parted like the Red Sea to let him into the center of their sweat-drenched circle. Zach had entered the center, and he never looked more fetching, donning nothing but jet-blue basketball shorts. "C'mon!" he cried, and soon Todd began dragging himself to the center, almost as if by an unconscious force. Next thing he new, he was there, facing Zach, with a sea of hungry, lusting eyes looking at every inch of his boyflesh. He slowly slipped out of his flips – it just seemed like the natural thing to do – and suddenly he saw himself at the first match. Gregg was getting ready to shout "Go!" when Todd stopped him. "Hold on, hold on, hold on!" Todd screamed. "Guys, I don't know what's going on… I… I just got here. I… I found Zach's thing about Foot Club and got intrigued and… I'm sorry, I don't know what I'm doing or even what's happening right now."

There was a pause. Gregg just smirked at him. "Well, you're about to find out what's happening. GO!"

3.

Zach began running at Todd and instantly tackled him to the ground. Todd, totally unaware of what was happening, soon sound himself horizontal in sand and panting for breath.

In the struggle, Zach was soon sitting on Todd's lap, then using his beautiful blond boyfeet to hold Todd's arms to the ground. With his free hands, Zach suddenly dug right into Todd's ribs. "OH MY GOD!" screamed Todd, the last word breaking like a laughed syllable. He had never been tickled in his life. He loved dishing it, he loved watching others get tickled, but he had never experienced this sensation. It's like electricity was being whipped inside his body, and it was nice… and terrible! Todd began laughing, but he couldn't stop! His emotions… they were being turned against him. He tried to move, but Zach's strong, powerful feet were driving his wrists into the ground. Todd couldn't believe it. He couldn't move. He tried bucking his hips but Zach's weight was too much for him. The fingers began crawling along his ribs and up to his armpits, and Todd began spasming hard. He was laughing and laughing and OH GOD HE COULDN'T STOP LAUGHING! He wanted to say something, provide a coherent argument as to why he didn't deserve this, but the tickles were short-circuiting his brain, destroying any chance to develop a thought or say a word.

He heard the faint sounds of the guys hooting and hollering around him, but Zach's perfectly stiff fingernails were turning Todd into a vessel for tickle ghosts to emerge. He couldn't believe it. He was helpless and laughing and getting more exhausted with each passing second. He wanted it to stop so badly but his massive, raging hardon was saying otherwise. No doubt Zach could feel it underneath him as he tortured the helpless Todd, but there seemed to be other things on his mind: turning Todd into a helpless Tickle Toy.

Time blurred, his senses got fucked up, and he couldn't tell how much time was actually passing during his tickle episode. He wanted to scream and pass out, but it was impossible. He then had a small burst of energy and mustered up a shout: "GOD, I GIVE UP!!" "You have to do better than that!" sneered Zach. "Whahahahat do you want me to haha say, Zach?!" "That you are my footslave!!" Without even thinking Todd screamed at the top of his lungs "I AM YOUR FOOTSLAVE ZACH!!"

It stopped.

It actually stopped. Todd couldn't believe it. His lungs were taking in bucket breaths, and then he turned onto his side, curled up in exhaustion. He had never been hornier in his life. As his head laid down on the sandy floor, he saw a virtual plethora of frat-toes gradually encroaching on him, and with weak breath just muttered a "feet..." before he passed out. He wasn't in shock, he just needed to sleep.

4.

Todd woke with toes in his mouth.

They weren't too far deep, but there was a salty taste right at the front of his lips. He tried to move. He couldn't. His hands were tied behind his back with zip-ties, and his ankles were bound together with the same. He moved a bit, and after a few seconds, realized he was completely naked. The toes drew out from his mouth and his blurry vision gradually came into something clear: Zach's sole was hovering above him. Zach was in a chair, and Todd was on the floor of some room of the fraternity, a cheap rug keeping his naked body from the plywood. He moved his head around – there was music in the background, guys were drinking, but their attire hadn't changed. They were all proudly barechested and barefooted, and even though he was embarrassed to be nude, Todd felt his cock twitch just a bit.

"Hey everyone!" shouted Gregg, "Zach's Tickle Toy just woke up!"

The guys standing around soon sat down, and Zach could see clearly now: he was in a small room, where two couches were facing each other against the near walls, and inbetween the couches (on either side) were chairs, one which housed Zach and one which housed Gregg. Todd, horrifically, was at the center of all this, about a dozen pairs of bared and sandaled feet on each side of him, only a foot away. Todd's cock twitched again. Todd tried moving one more time, but he was toast: there was nothing he could do.

"What's going on?" asked the weak, still-recovering Todd.

Zach just laughed. "You're in hell now, my friend."

"What happened?"

"I dunno," started Zach. "Hey Bill – mind playing back that footage?" Out of the corner of his eye, Todd could tell that some guy was at a computer in the corner of the room, and Todd thought he could see the YouTube logo on one of the pages there. Some buttons were pressed, and then out of the tinny computer speakers, he could hear his own voice scream out "I AM YOUR FOOTSLAVE ZACH!" Then it all came back to him. Oh shit.

"Yeah," started Zach. "Up for one hour and already gained 200 hits. You're a cel-web-rity, footslave!" Todd just groaned, half-out of worry, half-out of exhaustion. "So," Zach continued "we broke out the beers and got some time here. I wanted to ask you a few questions, footslave. Why'd you come here tonight?" The embarrassment was seeping in. "I'd rather not say…" started Todd. "C'mon!" started the guys on the couches. Their toes began prodding Todd, writhing around on the floor, helplessly bound. Some guys just wanted to poke Todd's helpless ribs. Some were wiggling their toes into his flesh, making him laugh, while a few just wanted to fondle their new erotic plaything. It was like an army of sweaty college feet had been unleashed on the poor boy all at once, hounds from hell traced on his nervous sweat. The twitch was even bigger this time 'round.

"Not a good answer, Todd…" sneered Gregg. "Now tell us… why did you come here tonight?"

Todd blurted out "I have a foot fetish! I'm sorry, I just… god, I just… I have a major foot fetish, guys. There. I said it."

"Really?" stated one of the anonymous guys on the couch. "Zach, make him prove it."

"With pleasure," Zach said. "Footslave! Sniff that foot!" The guy on the couch was extending his meaty size 10, and soon the toes were practically walking on Todd's face, the foot slithering its way up to Todd's nose. Todd didn't even hesitate: his instincts made him take a deep, amorous sniff of the guy's foot, and it smelled glorious. Sweaty, cheesy, and altogether tasty. His hips moved in accordance, and suddenly Todd could feel the eyes of a dozen or so guys all focused on his crotch. He didn't have time to get embarrassed – he just whiffed again. And again. And thrusted both times, subconsciously. He was immediately turned on.

"Wow," started Zach "Dude… you might have it even worse than I do." Todd heard this through yet another sniff. He could then feel another random foot starting to play with his third leg…

"Fuck, I love feet" Todd blurted out, without thinking. "Wow," started Gregg "This guy is a TOTAL footbitch. This is sensational! Hey Evan, start worshipping his soles."

Suddenly, the still-sniffing Todd felt some guy's mouth encompassing his pinkie toe on his left bound foot, and then working its way to the others. That foot on his crotch was having fun, and before long he found himself sucking really, really hard on the toes he was smelling just seconds ago. More feet landed on his chest and just began moving around. Some guys got down to the floor and began lightly tickling him on his ribs, legs, and crotch. Todd was going into pleasure overload, as everything he could ever want was happening right then and there. His ticklish body soon turned into one big orgasm, and as he thrust his last burst out, splaying the room, he could feel the heat in the room escalate, and some of the couch guys getting down on their knees with their fingers drawn. Soon, everything was becoming a blur – there was lots of tickling, lots of feet, lots of worshipping, all while the frat boys gradually began feeding the newfound slave nothing but beer and bong hits. Todd's body was exhausted beyond belief, but he was still horny, and the guys just couldn't stop using him. They were entranced.

Todd was soon licking feet in sandals, answering embarrassing fetish related questions, and kept catching the glimpses of camera flashes coming from unknowing directions. It was like a druggy haze, fantastic and confusing all at once. He lost track of how many times he came – and yes, it was that good.

5.

Light was peaking through the window of the room – daybreak. All the guys around him were now passed out on the floor or on the couches, some with each others' feet in their open, sleeping mouths. Todd was still awake, still underneath Zach's chair, sucking on his master's toes like the world's best lollipop, all while Zach was gradually edging himself towards a climax. When he came (and Todd could feel Zach's toes clench in his warm mouth as he did so), Zach soon sighed, and just froze for a bit. Even Todd stopped worshipping his classmates' perfect soles, and just laid there, still bound (the zip-ties no doubt having made an impression on his wrists and ankles from all the struggling), and soon hearing Zach's voice saying "c'mon – get dressed." Scissor snip. Scissor snip. The bonds were undone. Zach threw Todd's clothes – flips included – right at his face, and demanded again he get dressed. Todd did so at an exhausted snail's pace, but Zach didn't rush him. When Todd looked up at him, he had a look of acknowledgement from Zach: saying that "yeah, I beat you, but I was in your place once." Todd felt better, somehow.

Next thing he knew, Zach was slowly helping Todd walk back to his dorm. No words were said – the slap of their sandals against their heels in the damp morning air said enough. Todd reached into his pocket and pulled out his cell phone – he had signed up for Facebook

Mobile, and had discovered that he had just been tagged in 44 new photos. There was absolutely no going back at this point.

As Todd got back to his dorm, Zach turned to him and smiled. "You did great, mate," he started. "Really – you're awesome." "Thanks," whispered back Todd, weakly. "Any questions?", asked Zach. Todd thought, and could only come up with one: "Yeah… when's the next meeting?" Zach leaned and whispered into his ear "the date and time is written all over your chest." Todd really didn't remember, but knew Zach wasn't lying.

Todd opened the door to his room, aware of the sound of Doug's snoring. He sat down at his computer, and just reeled over all that happened. The he looked up – the TV was still roaring quietly, but Doug's feet were propped up on the footrest of their couch… and they were bared.

They were prefect. Todd drew closer. Size 10. Softest soles in the world. He brought his nose to the base of the toes, inhaled, and felt himself spring to life all over again. He tried to remember all the feet that he had worshipped in the past 6 hours, but nothing hit him as hard as this. This is what he had wanted to see for months, and now that those perfect feet were in front of him, and they were everything he could imagine and more. He listened. Doug was still snoring. After all he had just gone through – Todd's inhibitions were gone.

Without thinking, he went and began lightly sucking on Doug's perfect, glorious toes. He felt great. He was alive again, feeling like invincible steel. In a matter of seconds, his worshipping went from simple to passionate, and was soon engulfing the feet with his mouth, savoring every salty molecule. He was so engaged, he didn't even notice that Doug stopped snoring. He did notice this, though:

"Dude… what are you doing?"

Todd looked at Doug – he was wide awake. His tone was more curious than vindictive, but here Todd was: caught red-handed in his horny pursuit of the perfect foot to worship. "I… I'm sorry, Doug. I just… I have a foot fetish and I've been wanting to see your feet for so long and I would've given anything to worship them and just acted. I'm really, really sorry."

There was a pause.   Doug cocked his eyebrow, and asked *"Anything?"*

And Todd was found out, his greatest weakness suddenly exposed at the moment he least expected it, realizing now that he would be a perpetual footslave to the person who he thought would least control him… and there was nothing he could do about it.

Perhaps this is why it was the start to the greatest day of his life.

AFFLUENT

One for the foot-fetish kids.

There was now pounding against Kyle's locked door. "Open up!" the voices shouted. He scrambled about his room, trying to find a place to hide, a way out, just anything. He was panicking and desperate for a solution. "Hold on, I got a key" he heard from outside his solid-oak dorm room door. Kyle reached for his wallet... it was empty. He was just about ready to cry, as he knew what was going to happen next: he was going to be tickled for hours and hours and hours, and Kyle hated being the most ticklish person he had ever known...

———

Kyle loved guys feet. He had since he was a kid.

Growing up in a small New Jersey suburb, he never was afforded opportunities for wild dates with hot girls or ample spin-the-bottle games with junior high classmates. When he was around 12, his sexual awakening occurred when he was playing with his best friend at his house while his mom was at work some sunny summer weekday. In the den (where the big screen TV was located), Kyle and his friend Dylan sat on the same couch, their heads on opposite ends, their bared feet situated near each other. Though a new episode of *Power Rangers* was just starting up, Kyle, for whatever reason, just couldn't help but stare at Dylan's toes. That faint wisp of hair growing on top of them, the way the tips were perfectly rounded... they looked... delicious. He began rubbing Dylan's feet just out of nowhere, and though his dusty haired friend first looked at him with a cocked eyebrow, Dylan didn't say a word, largely because his head began tilting back and his eyes began to close: that look of genuine, powerful relaxation. Kyle kept it up, and it wasn't long before Dylan began sleeping and then snoring. Deep snoring.

Kyle moved Dylan's boy feet around a bit to try and wake him – no luck. Cracking a bit of a devious smile, Kyle tried something else: he ran his fingernail up Dylan's perfect left sole – and though the toes clenched a bit, Dylan continued snoring. His interest piqued, Kyle repositioned himself on the floor next to the couch, his arms wrapped around the sides of the sleeping Dylan's legs. He drew his face towards the base of Dylan's toes, and inhaled. The smell – that slightly pungent, colorful, yet undeniably delicious smell – is what changed Kyle's life. He had never been so... attracted to something. With the dense, guttural snores still filling up the den, Kyle then took the risk of his life: he opened his mouth and clenched his wet lips around Dylan's unconscious toes. He sucked and slurped them up like his foot was a giant lollipop, Kyle's drive soon taking over and turning this experience into a passionate foot worship section. Saliva was still dripping down Dylan's soles by the time Kyle was done a half-hour later. Almost as soon as he finished, though, Dylan woke up, still tired from his relaxed sleep. When asked what happened during the past hour, all Kyle could say is that the Red Ranger destroyed a giant squid monster in the second episode.

Kyle thought about that definitive moment a lot, but he thought of it even more so now that he was entering college. His foot fetish had gotten him into a lot of trouble in high school, but it also gave him a lot of pleasure. He never was attracted to guys: just their feet. Yet, really, that was enough for him: he had constructed his whole sexual life around that one small aspect, yet it was enough to fill up his masturbatory fantasies a dozen times over – he saw no need for change. Now, as he stood with bags of clothes hanging from his shoulders, he couldn't help but notice the never-ending supply of guys walking around in baggy shorts in flip-flops, or jeans while barefoot, or khakis with sneakers and no-show ankle socks. His parents had officially said their goodbyes about an hour ago, and now he was on his own: in the land of temptation.

Having finally found his room (and finally gotten his keys to work), Kyle entered the surprisingly spacious little space that he would be living in for the next year. Much to Kyle's surprise, however, was that half the room was already filled up. There was an empty, generic bed on one side (adjacent to a closet and an empty computer desk), and on the other, there was a laundry hamper, a small circular table in the shape of a yin-yang (likely bought at Target), a desk with a new Mac all up and running, and a TV sitting atop up-turned milk-carton boxes on the far wall. Kyle turned to his left, and saw the most handsome sight he had ever seen in his life: a 19-year-old boy in just his shorts, with a chiseled set of abs, buzz-cut-short hair, and the most gorgeous size-13s he had ever seen. Kyle thought he was going to die.

"So… you must be Kyle."

Kyle didn't know what to say – he was still in a trance, his cock twitching ever-so-slightly through his boxers, as if his mind had shut down because he was stuck in some sort of erotic coma.

"Hello? You there?"

The muscular Adonis was still addressing him.

"Oh, sorry," started Kyle. "I'm… Kyle."

"It's OK, man. I space out too, sometimes. I'm Matt."

They shook hands. Kyle set his stuff down next to the empty bed.

"So…" he started, "you're already here."

"Ha ha, yeah. I'm on the swim team here – I got a scholarship just for swimming, but even though it's not in season, the coach wanted all the water athletes here early for evaluations and an early test meet in October. I think it's stupid, personally – you shouldn't have to swim when it's less than 60 degrees outside, but, whatever. I'm here, and I'm set up. Decided to take this side, hope you don't mind."

"Oh, no – not at all" stammered Kyle. "I can imagine there being quite the demand for swimmers now, given Michael Phelps and all."

"Dude!" started Matt, swinging his legs off the bed, "I know! That guy is such a fucking badass. I was watching him all summer – dude knows what he's doing. I swear to god his toes are webbed or something."

Kyle, of course, couldn't keep his eyes off of Matt's feet, as hard as he tried. Kyle looked up and saw Matt caught his footwards stare. Kyle thought fast:

"Well, yours aren't. Webbed that is."

Matt laughed.

"Ha ha, nah. These clod-hoppers get their job done, though." He pounced off the bed and slipped on his cheap, black, plastic flip-flops. "Yeah, they've helped me win quite the few matches – and can kick like hell during a fight. Anywho, I'm gonna get some food. I'll catch you later."

In a flash, the bare-chested, sandal-clad Matt had snagged a shirt from his closet and closed the door behind him. Kyle checked: as far as he knew, he hadn't moved an inch from where he first saw Matt's perfect young body. Minutes must have passed since the door closed, as Kyle just stood in amazement. Was this really going to be who he was rooming with? Jesus – this was just so unreal. Instead of worrying about unpacking, though, Kyle's eyes darted towards Matt's closet, and his impulses took over: he opened the door up and looked in the laundry basket: it was empty aside from a few shirts. Matt hadn't donned socks yet – he must've been wearing flip-flops from the second he got there. Either way, Kyle's mind was already awash with possibilities…

As Kyle had settled in during the first week, he gradually got to learn more about the perpetually unshod Matt: grew up in Montana, had a fondness for the swimming pool at the YMCA when he turned 14 and had been drawn to it ever since. He had a girlfriend back home, but she knew that Matt was a bit of a flirt: they were just in an "open relationship" which, of course, meant that they were going to break up soon. Kyle found this all utterly fascinating, and even when doing tasks like registering for classes, still kept thinking about Matt's feet. He wasn't one to get obsessed over someone easy – after all, he was at college, and there was a literal buffet of footflesh at his eyes – but he kept thinking back to Matt's unstoppably lickable monster feet. By the end of that first week, it was settled: he had to worship them.

As classes started, Kyle began settling into a groove (he decided to pursue classes in both Creative Writing and Philosophy this first term), and began making a few easy acquaintances. He was happy with how normal it all seemed initially (aside from the cafeteria thing, where he was able to indulge the whim of every tastebud he had). As Wednesday rolled around, Kyle felt he had an easy day: by 7PM, he had already finished his reading for Intro to Philosophy and just did a huge rewrite on his assignment for his creative non-fiction class, so he felt he deserved a break. He sat in his bed and began watching Matt's TV. As Conan just began finishing up his opening monologue a few hours later, the door to Kyle's room opened with a violent bang.

Kyle whipped around quick enough to see Matt hurl his backpack against the wall in complete rage. "I CAN'T BELIEVE THIS!!" he shouted, soon pounding his fists on his mattress. "THIS IS SUCH BULLSHIT!!" Kyle was worried, and tried to calm him down.

"Matt, buddy – what happened?"

"I'll tell you what happened!" he started, decked out in a plain white T-shirt, black shorts, and those ever-present flips. "Coach is letting Orton take the lead spot at the meet in October! I'm so pissed off!!"

"Why's that a bad thing?" inquired Kyle.

"'cos I'm a better swimmer than he is! I beat him by two whole seconds on the 100m! It makes no goddamn sense that coach would favor someone slower than me. Goddammit!"

Matt – running out of inanimate objects to throw – picked up one of his flip-flops and threw it at Kyle's bed. It landed next to Kyle's pillow, but Kyle didn't have time to notice as he saw Matt angrily flop down on his bed. Matt shoved his face in his pillow and was breathing heavily. This continued for a minute.

Suddenly, something came over Kyle. A sort of strange bravery that he hadn't felt before. He didn't have time to analyze the should-I-or-shouldn't-I factor because it all happened so fast: next thing he knew, he was sitting on Matt's bed. Suddenly, Kyle spoke with confidence.

"Dude – you got to calm down. Now, who's this Orton guy?"

"Phil", Matt uttered through his pillow. "Phil Orton. He's a senior and a douchebag."

Without hesitating, Kyle put his hands on Matt's downturned feet, and put them in his lap.

"Turn over" ordered Kyle. Matt, angry with the world, did so without even thinking, Matt now staring at the ceiling while Kyle positioned Matt's feet right in his lap. He slowly put his hands to Matt's beautiful, enormous, perfect feet and began rubbing them, talking to Matt the whole time.

"Well, look at it this way, Matt: Phil a jerk but he's also a senior – of course he's going to get preferential treatment. That's just the way shit happens. If you're already beating the star senior's time, though, don't you think coach is noticing?" At this point, Kyle's hands began massaging deeper and deeper, enough to where he could physically see Matt's tension drip off of his shoulders. "Dude, this isn't even the real season: that's gonna start happening in the spring. Phil's only here one more year: let the dude have his time in the sun. God knows you're going to get more chances. You really can't sweat the small stuff, 'cos really it's going to bring you down in the end."

There was a good few minutes that passed as Kyle's hands kneaded Matt's smooth, uncaloused soles in the silence. Matt, finally, spoke.

"Dude… you're right. I mean, I'm still angry, but you're right: this isn't the only chance I'll ever have. I'm just starting off. Let the little fuckwad have his spotlight – I'll be stealing it soon enough anyways."

"That's the spirit!"

"Oh, and dude… where did you learn that shit?"

"What?" asked Kyle.

"That foot massage stuff. I mean… it feels fucking incredible."

"Well… self-taught I guess. Had lots of practice, you could say."

"What, with guy's feet?"

"Yeah."

Oh shit. Kyle blurted out that "yeah" without even thinking about it. Blood was already rushing to his soon-blushing cheeks, but he kept working Matt's feet as if nothing happened.

"… so, what, you got like a foot fetish or something?"

"Yeah." Dammit, there it goes again.

"Like, all feet or…"

"No, just guys feet. It's kind of weird."

Matt was growing a bit uncomfortable, but wasn't saying anything about it.

"So… OK… in your perfect little world, what would you be doing to my feet right now?"

"Well, to be honest… I'd be sucking in your toes, and licking your soles, and just making your feet feel good, really."

"I… see." Matt was definitely uncomfortable with this now. Yet as he still held onto those feet, Kyle knew he couldn't let this opportunity slip away.

"Is… is that something you'd like to try?" asked Kyle.

"What? You sucking my toes?"

"Yeah."

"Um, no thanks dude. I mean, the footrub is great, but…"

"What if I paid you?"

Again, Kyle caught himself saying something without thinking. He looked at Matt. Matt's eyebrow was cocked with interest.

"How much?"

"Um… $20?"

Matt mulled this around for a second.

"So let's get this straight" he started: "YOU would be paying ME for the chance to suck on MY toes, correct?"

"Um… yeah." replied Kyle.

There was a pause.

"Let's see the cash."

In a second, Kyle had jumped off the bed, gone over to the desk, and reached for his wallet. He pulled out a crisp $20 and walked over and handed it to Matt. Matt readjusted himself, flexed his feet, then just laid back and closed his eyes. "Alright man – go for it."

This was it! Kyle was stunned this was even happening at all. He kneeled at the foot of Matt's bed so that those perfect size 13s were inches from his face. He put his nose up to the base of the big toe on his right foot and inhaled. This, thought Kyle, is what heaven smells like. His erection – stirring since he ever put his hand on Matt's foot – felt like steel thunder right about now: rock hard and eager to do something about it.

Kyle still lightly massaged Matt's gargantuan feet, but then made the risky move and began sucking on Matt's big toe. Matt clenched a bit at first, holding his breath, but then Matt released it and said "OK. Cool." all with his eyes still closed. Kyle's mouth slowly slid across the tip of the toes, across the toe nail, around past those wiry small hairs at the base of his toe, and then back again. Each toe was a treat unto itself, a sweet savory delight that was treated with the greatest care and tender worshipping respect. Kyle's horny mind was losing track of time. It wasn't long before all 10 toes had undergone a similar treatment, and Kyle's tongue began slowly tracing the outline of Matt's soles from the heels on upward. Kyle's favorite part were still the tops of the feet, as that's where all the nerves tended to be. There were faint bits of hair on them as well, but that just kept driving Kyle onward. He was passionately making out with these feet, and it was utterly glorious. He then went back to the toes, and began sucking on them in a rhythmic fashion, up and down, slowly yet surely. Matt's mid-section arched up, and Kyle glanced: Matt had been jacking himself off for the past few minutes! With that in mind, Kyle kept at it, Matt soon began moaning, and right as the young swimmer came, Kyle could feel those toes clench while in his mouth – which was enough to make Kyle come inside his boxers. He went back to slowly, lightly massaging those feet as Matt lay there, a trail of sperm lining up his white shirt. After a second, Matt withdrew his feet and sat cross-legged on his bed. Kyle looked up, and Matt grabbed Ky by the chin and brought him face to face.

"Listen" Matt started, "you do not tell anyone about what just happened, OK? ANYONE! That is strictly between you and me."

Kyle stammered "Dude, it's OK. It'll be our secret."

Matt frowned "… that's not good enough, dude."

"I'm ticklish" Kyle blurted out. "Listen, I'm really, really ticklish and I fucking hate being tickled, as it makes me feel weak and totally powerless. That's my secret. You can have that one."

Matt stared quixotically. "That's your secret? I could tell the guys on the team that and they would just…"

"NO!!!" shouted Kyle. "Don't tell anyone!! The second you point out that someone's ticklish to someone, what do they do? They tickle that person! I can't stand being tickled, OK! I'm telling you that in confidence, alright?"

Matt smirked "OK. Fair deal. Now if you don't mind, I'm gonna get ready for bed."

Two hours later, the lights were turned out in the dark, and a few minutes passed. Kyle then spoke up.

"Hey Matt?"

"What?"

"Would you mind if we did that again… sometime?"

There was a pause.

"You got $20 on you?"

"Yeah."

"… then sure."

Kyle slept very, very well that night.

A week later, it was Thursday, and Kyle didn't have any classes that day. This meant, of course, that he could sleep in. He hadn't worshipped Matt's feet since then, but it was OK: they were still on good standing. Kyle was actually dreaming about doing that very act when he was awoken by hard pounding on the door. Kyle tried to ignore it, but it was quite persistent. He got up – in his boxers – and opened the door. It was a 6'5" Polish guy in long-sleeves, jeans, and flips, his back-pack slung over his shoulder.

"Um, can I help you?" started Kyle.

"Hi, I'm Will. I'm on the swim-team with Matt."

"Oh, hi."

"So… you're the guy?"

"… what are you talking about?"

"The foot guy."

Kyle stood with his mouth agape. Matt had told the guys on the team about his roommate with the foot fetish. He couldn't believe it.

"Um… well, yeah. That's me, I guess."

"OK, sweet."

Will just moved his way into the room. Confused, Kyle closed (and locked) the door. After absorbing the flavor of the room in a bit, Will set down his backpack, kicked off his flip-flops, and sat on Matt's bed.

"OK," Will started, "how do we do this?"

"Um, dude… I honestly don't know what you're talking about."

"Oh, I thought Matt explained it to you. He said that if any guy on the team needed a foot massage to go see his roommate, and if we wanted to make $20, we could as long as you got to suck on our toes for awhile."

"Well, suck on toes AND lick your soles" Kyle said in a non-chalant way that surprised even him.

"Alright, well sign me up!" Will adjusted himself and awaited for his feet to be serviced. Kyle was still a bit stunned.

"Will, was it? Listen, it's not that simple…"

"It's OK – I can wait."

Kyle had this opportunity in front of him. This stunning, perfect, opportunity. He didn't know what to think. Yet, though he wasn't sure, it sounded like Will wasn't clear on specifics. Kyle, technically, could do whatever he wanted. So... he did. As Will laid there in barefooted anticipation, Kyle slowly slid off his boxers, leaving him naked. He bent down, and picked up one of Will's canvas-soled flip-flops. Must be size 12, he thought. He took a big whiff of where the sweatblackened toe imprints were, and he went from zero-to-horny in a nanosecond. He looked at the perfect Polish feet sticking out of those thin blue jeans, and just dug in.

Seconds after Will had jerked himself off to the intense foot erotica he was experiencing (some two hours later), Kyle heard his door knocking again. Dripping pre-cum, he was a bit nervous, but the door kept pounding. "Be back in one second" he told Will. Will was too blissed out to notice. Nude, Kyle slowly, carefully cracked open the door while concealing his hardon. "Hello?"

A short, stocky young guy stood there: about 5'6", a bit of muscle mass on him, gloriously jet-dark hair. "Hey, are you the foot guy?"

"Oh, hey Greg!" shouted Will. "It's OK. I'm just finishing up."

"Sweet" said Greg, just walking into the room as if it were his. He turned and saw the nude Kyle still sporting a raging erection. "Heh heh – looks like you still got some juice in ya!"

Will slid back into his flips and began making his way out, before he stopped himself. "Oh, pfft. Sorry – stupid me: you got the $20?"

Kyle was dumbfounded yet again, yet non-hesitant: "Um, yeah, it's right over here."

He handed Will a $10 and two $5's, as he was out of $20's. Will thanked him as he walked out the door and Greg began removing his Skechers. "Do you want me to keep my socks on or not?"

This was already too much, yet Kyle couldn't (or perhaps wouldn't) do a thing to change it.

―――――――――

Two weeks later, Kyle had serviced just about every single guy on the swim team (but was told there were already a few holdouts). Kyle was obviously a bit broke, but he sure as hell didn't mind. This week he was looking for an off-campus job to help feed his fetish, but at the same time he was endearing himself to the swim clique. He had gone out for a few late night Taco Bell runs with them, and he was becoming a bit socially acclimated to this group of fun, hard-partying guys that – even in the middle of September – still donned flip-flops like there was no tomorrow. Kyle was elated when he found out he was invited to the party at Phil's apartment that weekend – it was exactly what Kyle was expecting in terms of fun college experiences.

When that fateful Friday night rolled around, Kyle walked there with Matt, both of them donning flips and in good spirits. Kyle was starting to develop feelings towards Matt that were a bit stronger than normal, but he still had only worshipped Matt's feet once (unlike Will, who had been back three additional times for foot worship, jokingly offering to service Kyle's feet on the last visit). When they got to Phil's apartment (off-campus, of course), it was around 11:30PM, and there were already gloriously drunken sorority girls there, and half the swim team was either starting to drink or trying to kick each other's ass at Wii Olympics. Kyle actually got to talk to a lot of the swim guys about non-foot stuff, too: the new Coen Brothers movie, if the Arcade Fire was really going to play a show at the end of the term on campus, etc.

In fact, Kyle's role as a foot service toy didn't even come up. Yet, there was one swimmer he hadn't met yet: Phil. He finally did (after a few vodka shots), and it was just as bad as he envisioned it: Phil was tall, commanding, an egomaniac, and – as seemed to be the team requirement – donning flip-flops, exposing the biggest set of feet that Kyle had ever seen. It was like he had been starving for a year and someone just plopped the biggest sirloin steak in the world right in front of him, served on cheap Old Navy flip-flops: the meatiest, thickest, most glorious feet he had ever seen. Phil did mention "Oh, hey, you're the Foot Guy!" and even wiggled his toes a bit at Kyle, but was soon distracted by new pledge Stephanie, who was flirting with him across the room. As he walked away, Kyle couldn't get those big-toed monsters out of his mind, but was soon brought up into a game of Wii Shot Put, and lost track of time for the next hour or so.

By the time Kyle had finished up, he had to pee like no tomorrow (all that booze goes down fast). He stumbled to the restroom, and as he was washing his hands after, he heard the unpleasant whining of a girl in the room adjacent. As he stepped out of the restroom, Stephanie was slamming the door behind her.

"Hey, you alright?"

"Jeez – no!" Stephanie didn't seem upset, but wasn't pleased.

"What's wrong?"

"Pfft, Phil – he began making out with me and the passed out HALF-WAY THROUGH. He's now just lying there snoring like the Jolly Green Giant or something. God, I hate it when he drinks. If you see Carol, tell her I went back to my place."

Kyle had never met a Carol, and certainly wouldn't know what she'd look like if he did. Stephanie was out of there in a flash, and he turned to see that the rest of the team was eagerly watching the current Wii Baton Relay. Perhaps it was the booze, the lack of inhibitions, or just caught up in the whirlwind week he'd been having, but Kyle took a risk. He sneaked into the room Stephanie had just come out of: it was Phil's bedroom, and it was pitch black (it was about 2AM by Kyle's estimations). He locked the door behind him, and turned to hear the loud snoring of the Jolly Green Giant himself, facedown on his bed with his gargantuan feet sticking out over the edge. Since his bed was just two mattresses stacked on top of each other on the floor, Kyle noticed that Phil's toes were just inches from the floor. "What the hell," Kyle thought.

Kyle laid facedown on the floor at the foot of the mattresses, the gigantic toes just an inch from his mouth. Like a fish reaching for bait, Kyle slowly reached up and began sucking on Phil's toes, though at first Kyle was blown away by the strong, glorious odor that permeated from those monster soles. Still drunk, Kyle didn't mind. In fact, he got a little sloppy, his tongue lavishing Phil's soles with an almost reckless abandon. He'd stop every 30 seconds or so just to make sure Phil was still snoring, but after 5 times, he figured that Phil was out cold. God, these feet were so tasty and big and hot-looking and – at the moment – HIS! Kyle unzipped his jeans to make sure he was well-stroked while worshipping the god-like feet before him. Slowly, gradually jacking it while his tongue absorbed every molecule that existed between Phil's toes. Slowly, he was coming to what was going to be the climax of his life…

"What the fuck are you doing?!"

Oh shit.

Phil had woken up. His slightly-turned head was staring at Kyle, whose mouth was dripping with satisfaction and whose cock was as solid as a rod and in plain sight.

"Oh, no you didn't." uttered Phil.

Kyle didn't need anything more than that. He zipped up as quick as he could and bolted right out the door… almost knocking over Matt who was passing by outside.

"Fuck dude! What's wrong with you?" started Matt.

"Dude was licking my feet while I was asleep!" shouted Phil from his bedroom.

All the other guys were mulling about, having won their Wii Medals. They now all turned towards the developing situation.

Matt turned to Kyle "Oh, you're in deep shit now. You might have to owe him more than $20 man."

Kyle shouted "I don't have any money on me!"

"What about that I.O.U. you promised me last time?" shouted Will, who did not get paid during his last session.

"It's OK," started Matt to the group, slyly; "there's another way we can extract payment from Kyle."

"What?"

"Kyle once told me that he's ticklish…"

Kyle's eyes widened to the size of dinner plates. Next thing he knew, he was running as fast as he could back to his room.

His breath was panicked in the cool night air, his sandals preventing him from breaking a full running stride. He didn't need to turn around – he could hear the hurried sounds of the slapping flip-flops of an entire swim team not far behind him. This was impossible. This wasn't happening… yet it was deserved: he had just broken the unspoken rules to his "agreement" with that swim team. He just wanted to go to sleep right now and wake up all safe and in his room with all of this behind him… but that wasn't going to happen. Kyle got to his dorm room and locked it, turning off all the lights.

There was now pounding against Kyle's locked door. "Open up!" the voices shouted. He scrambled about his room, trying to find a place to hide, a way out, just anything. He was panicking and desperate for a solution. "Hold on, I got a key" he heard from outside his solid-oak dorm room door. Kyle reached for his wallet… it was empty. He was just about ready to cry, as he knew what was going to happen next: he was going to be tickled for hours and hours and hours, and Kyle hated being the most ticklish person he had ever known…

"HERE HE IS!" said Matt as the door swung open, keys in his hand. In a flash, the guys had pounced on Kyle and were holding him down to the floor. Kyle began pleading: "Please! I'm sorry! It was just the one time! I swear!!"

In response, he heard an inordinate amount of angry profanities, but Matt played it cool and addressed all.

"Guys! You know what, it's OK. Kyle did something stupid. We've all done stupid stuff. Let's give him a bit of a break, alright? Does that sound OK, Kyle?"

"Yeah" Kyle gulped.

"But," continued Matt, "wouldn't it be fair that Phil get some revenge for what you did to him? Wouldn't that balance things out a bit?"

Kyle nodded in agreement.

"Me too!" shouted Will, almost as an afterthought.

"Yeah, you too, Will" continued Matt, who then turned behind him. "Phil, trust me: the kid is very ticklish. It's your call."

Phil donned the most diabolical shit-eating grin Kyle had ever seen. He was in a room with about 8 swim-team guys who were going to obey his every order. This was not good.

"Lock the door" started Phil. "And make him naked." The guys didn't remove Kyle's clothes – they ripped them off him, making them unusable ever again. Soon, there were four guys holding down his arms and legs, leaving Kyle naked, spread-eagled, and totally helpless. Phil pulled over Kyle's desk chair and sat right between his legs, putting Phil's toes just inches from Kyle's exposed balls. Kyle's erection had faded due to absolute fear. Phil was loving this.

"First, Kyle," started the Swim God, "I want to see how horny my feet really make you." He then lifted up his bared monstrosities and placed them square on Kyle's chest, the big toes right at his nipples, rubbing them slightly. "You like that, don't you?" The feet began slowly circling Kyle's ribcage, and he couldn't help but be a bit turned on. "Yeah… tell me how much you like them." Kyle screamed "They're the best feet I have ever worshipped in my whole life!!"

"That's what you told me!" shouted Will. "And me!" shouted Greg.

"Well," started Phil, "we just might have to have a test where Kyle gives us the real truth. Of his favorite feet." Kyle's hardon was returning. "But first," started, Phil, "I want to see just how ticklish he is…"

Phil's monster toes slowly began inching their way to Kyle's armpits, and the big toes began circling, tickling all of Kyle's armpit hairs. Kyle screamed with laughter, deliciously horny laughter. Without orders, one of the guys sitting at his feet began tickling his left foot. "No, not my feet!!" shouted Kyle. Phil looked over. "Oh, Andy already is getting in on the fun. Hey – let's **all** get in on the fun!" Then, the wiggling, tormenting, fingers of a ton of guys descended on Kyle's naked, sensitive body. They were tickling the space between his ribs, the nape of his neck, his armpits, his thighs, his balls, and everywhere. He was instantly hard, begging. Will moved close to Kyle's sweaty head, placed his sweaty canvas flip-flop right to his face and said "Start licking!!" which Kyle was only able to do between huge gulps of laughter. As the horny tickling continued, the guys wound up enjoying it all the more, and soon more toes began tickling his body than fingers, and Kyle came right then and there. But that wasn't enough. As time began blurring together, he just remembered at one point he was ordered to suck on as many toes at once, judge feet by smell, and beg for more tickling as he was being tickled. He came twice, then three times, and then a fourth. By the fifth time (sucking on Phil's toes, again), he was shooting blanks, as all his sperm had been drained out of him. Then, Phil kneeled down to Kyle and began using his ultra-long fingernails and began scraping them slowly and gently along Kyle's sides. Kyle dry-shot again and then passed out.

———————

Kyle awoke with a foot in his mouth. The unconscious foot of Phil. It tasted grand.

Kyle was still nude and wearing enough dried cum for an entire orgy. He looked around. The guys – all of them – had passed out at one point or another, and now they were all in Matt/Kyle's room. Kyle smirked a bit when he saw that Will had passed out with Andy's feet in his mouth. Kyle tried to move… but he couldn't. His arms were tied to the radiator and his legs to the foot of his bed. Kyle didn't remember any of this. Then he heard a bit of a digital ring. It was text message sent to his phone. Will woke up, the phone in his hand (what was Kyle's phone doing in Will's possession, pray tell?). Will groggily removed Andy's size 9's from his mouth, and looked at the text message. He then turned to the still-bound, still-nude, unbelievably horny Kyle. Will spoke out loud.

"HEY DUDE, I'M IN TOWN, SURPRISE SURPRISE – that's a text message for you, Ky. Um… who's Dylan?"

THE AD

The two tales that follow have the most interesting backstory of all. I had been posting some of my early works on one awesome tickle-related internet forum, and it wasn't long before the head admin contacted me personally, asking about a commission. I was intrigued, but even more so by his request: some years ago, a writer named Mark Apoapsis had written a tale called "ROFL, Inc.", which, basically, was about an institute where people paid (via the internet) to tickle real-life guys with specially-designed lasers. This admin was looking for an unofficial sort of "prequel" to the events of that story, and I obliged, very flattered that he trusted me with a project so personal. The response to this was so overwhelming, I did a sequel to this prequel called "The Lickle", which follows. Oh, it was a challenge, but boy was it fun...

Andy's eyes burst wide open. This wasn't supposed to happen.

Here he was, his body wrapped around that of his opponent, their feet grinding into the soft padding of his college's wrestling pit, Andy in the middle of the tryout of his life. He was pitted against a junior named Steve who got on the wrestling team his freshman year, and the eyes of the current team, the coach, and all the other potential frosh wrestlers were all over his body, currently tense and rigid – Steve wasn't moving an inch. With Andy's arms wrapped around Steve's waist, Steve's hands were placed strategically right in the middle of Andy's ribs, and that's where it happened: the fingers squeezed in, digging ever-so-softly into Andy's flesh, and – with that – Andy was being tickled. He laughed, his ribcage folded in, and Steve made his move, using Andy's second of vulnerability to his advantage, flipping the freshman around and pinning him on the ground. There were some cheers from the stands – Steve's buddies no doubt. With that, Andy's fate was sealed: he wasn't going to make the team this year, and, breathless on the mat, he was still grinning; not because he wanted to, but that one squeeze still had its ticklish reverberations in his body, and he was smiling against his will. It was almost humiliating: Andy didn't make the team – because he was ticklish.

Instead of returning to the stands to watch the rest of the tryouts like everyone else, Andy simply got up and left, walking away angry and in a huff. This wasn't fair – he was supposed to be that all-star athlete that broke into a high-ranked NCAA wrestling team his first time out. God knows he dominated the sport back in high school – everyone back at home would be so disappointed that he didn't make it this year. Maybe he would just lie to them – but, no, they'd be following the rankings online. Shit. This just isn't fair.

Still only two weeks into his term, Andy determined that he already hated being in college. It wasn't that bad of an experience, really: he had a single, made some fast friends already, and was enjoying his classes so far, but the wrestling tryout had genuinely tainted his feelings about everything – he wasn't sure if he was in the mood to even eat tonight. A few people in passing asked how it went (god knows he talked this thing up enough amidst his friends), but he blew past them without acknowledging their presence. Andy could get rather emotional when things didn't go his way, and this, easily, ranked as one of those experiences.

He went back into his room to find Sophie checking her e-mail on his computer. "How'd it go?" his sweet girlfriend asked. Sophie flew in this week just to be here for the weekend and for Andy's tryouts, her short black hair still musty and messy, no doubt having just woke up in the past hour while Andy was at the morning tryouts.

"I didn't make it."

"What?" she shouted.

"I know – I didn't... I can't fucking believe I didn't make it."

"What happened?" she asked.

Andy thought about what to say. He contemplated telling her that he didn't make it 'cos he was tickled for a fraction of a second and he lost his composure... but he stepped around it carefully: "I dunno – other guy was just better than me."

Sophie arched her eyebrow – 'cos she knew Andy had beaten stronger guys than him before, but simply resigned and accepted it. "Well I'm sorry, babe."

Andy was finally able to glance at her figure, and she was still in just her bra and panties as before. She was still a spectacular girlfriend, and during this moment of weakness, Andy felt bad: how could a hot girl like that still be with him? He was broke as hell, up to the point where she paid for her own plane ticket out here. Andy wanted to be the guy that paid for her dinners and surprised her with jewelry and whatnot, but with his job scrubbing pots and pans after classes once a week, he could barely save enough to get by for seven days at a time. For someone as strong and macho as Andy was, this was always a sore spot for him.

"Well" Sophie started, almost purring out the word, "what do you want to do?"

Frustrated and exhausted, Andy looked at her and smiled, albeit faintly. He placed the toe of his left shoe against the heel of his right, and peeled his ankle-socked feet right out of his sneakers. He turned and flopped onto his bed and leveled with Sophie: "I honestly just want to lie down and forget this even happened."

"Mind if I lie with you?" she asked.

Smiling, Andy said "Sure – why not?"

———————

Around midnight, Sophie's head was nuzzling against Andy's bare chest, coming off of one of the better nights of sex they had ever had. Andy stroked her hair while she lightly caressed his chest. Even with her bra still on, she was still a gorgeous sight, and as she snuck out of the covers to put her panties back on, Andy slowly began slipping into post-coital bliss. Andy heard her fidgeting with something on his computer – possibly his mic, but he was too chill to even open his eyes to notice. As he felt was Sophie slowly working her way up his body into her original position, her warm body wrapped slowly into his.

Then, came the soft, coy question: "Hey Andy?"

"Yeah?"

"Are you… ticklish?"

Andy's eyes burst open, but it was too late – her nails began drawing lines in his armpits, and his muscled body spasmed and withered, his mouth open with the thoughts of vocalizing his protest to her actions, but, instead, all that came out was halting, high-pitched laughter. The tough wrestler was reduced to nothing by his girlfriends fingernails. "P-please!" he cried. "Stop!" Her infectious grin was growing with every passing second – she was enjoying Andy's reactions too damn much to stop.

In Andy's fevered, crazed mind, all he could think of was escape, because there was no way he could win this scenario: just a few tickles in and he was already down for the count. He tried folding his arms down to his sides, but her hands, spiderlike, were wedged into his body too well and nothing he could do could stop the ticklish onslaught. Finally, in a moment of brief courage, he managed to get his hands around her wrists and finally got her to stop. As he put her arms well out of distance, she laughed, pleased to know it actually took this much effort on his part to stop her. Andy tried to catch his breath, saving up cruel words for her on how never to do that again – but she just beamed at him happily. He let go of her wrists and watched as she collapsed her body around him. After a few minutes, she quietly dozed off to sleep, but Andy was still wide awake – not believing that twice in one day, he was reduced to nothing just by someone moving their fingers. Maybe Andy wasn't invincible afterall – maybe he, in fact, had a weakness.

The next day, after kissing Sophie goodbye as she went through airport security to head back home, Andy drove back to campus, pleased with how the weekend went… all things considered. When he got back to his room, he locked the door behind him as per usual. He sat at the chair in front of his computer, intent on checking his e-mail and – who knows – maybe even getting some homework done this weekend. The comp booted up, Andy reached into his mini-fridge to grab a beer (he wasn't of age, but who was gonna stop him in his single?), and he noticed a new file on his desktop: "AndyT.mp3" He clicked on it.

The computer mic was on last night – and suddenly Andy was reliving every single revolting minute of the tickle torture he received at the hands of his girlfriend. Here, captured in digital perfection, was Andy's torment. Each time Andy heard his own voice crack in desperation, a little something broke inside him, each crack revealing that he wasn't as macho as he thought he was. His girlfriend pays for stuff, he got tickled by a guy and lost his spot on the wrestling team, he was under a pile of homework – Andy got frustrated. In just a T-shirt and baggy silver athletic-shorts, Andy needed to go somewhere – anywhere! –

from here. He hurriedly slipped his feet into a pair of worn leather flip-flops and bolted out the door, totally unsure of where he would go.

He wound up wandering around campus a bit, eventually winding up in the dining hall, buying an apple just to have something to eat, and then going into the commons hall, unsure of what to do. He wound up just collapsing on one of the public couches right next to the main entrance, a few students walking past him to head off to the cafeteria and some to whatever meetings they had going on that day. Adam brought his head down and tapped his foot nervously. He glanced up at the bulletin board in front of him, and then he saw the ad. He saw three convincing words that couldn't have been for anyone else but him:

"Male?

Broke?

Ticklish?"

This couldn't be. No way. This was impossible. Andy glanced around and saw that no one was really paying attention to him. He picked himself up off the couch and walked to the bulletin board, eyeing the ad. No details. It was printed out on computer paper and the bottom was cut with scissors into little flaps – each one rippable and containing a single phone number. No names, no nothing. Andy glanced around him again, and, cautiously, grabbed one of those little flaps with the phone number on it and ripped it off. He glanced again – judging by the three missing tabs on the sheet, three other guys were already interested as well.

Andy calmly walked back to his room, his flips slapping against his soles and echoing across the quads on his way there. He kept glancing at the little flap of paper, curious. All it was was a phone number. His eyes kept coming back to it, staring at it as if, perhaps, there was some more information to be ascertained. But nothing. Just a number.

When Andy finally got back to his hall and locked his room door behind him, he sat on his bed for a moment, still staring at that little slip of paper. He reached towards his desk to pick up his cell phone, but hesitated. What the hell was he doing? He hated being tickled. Sure, he was desperate for money, but this desperate? It seemed a little much, even for him. But, really, what else was he to do? This seemed like the best out… so Andy took a deep breath… and dialed.

Ringing. "Hello, this is Mike!"

"Um, hi – this is Andy."

"Hello there Andy. Nice to meet you."

There was a slight pause. Andy started. "So, um, I saw your ad."

"Very nice to hear. So, I assume you fit those three characteristics?"

"Well, um, yeah, but I don't really know what you are or what the deal is or what here, 'cos…"

"Hold on there" stated Mike in a pleasing, simple voice. "Let me jump in 'cos I have no doubt you got a lot of questions. I run this company called ROFL, Inc. It's a high-tech, online company. Let me ask you Andy – you ever go online?"

"Yeah, like every day."

"Sweet. You ever go to porn sites?"

"Um, that's kind of a personal question…"

"So… that's a yes then?"

Andy hesitated a bit. "Yeah."

"Dude, it's OK. We all do it. Well, ROFL is, in essence, a porn site, but unlike other sites, this doesn't contain any nudity or sex or anything else like that."

"… so where do you call it a 'porn' site?"

"Andy, I assume you go to college here in town, right?"

"Yeah."

"Let me give you our address. Why don't you swing on by for a quick meeting."

"Dude, well, I dunno…"

"Oh man, I'm sorry – I don't mean to creep you out, Andy. It's not like my basement or anything – we're actually located in the business district not to far from where your school is at. Oh, and just as a sign of good faith, there's going to be $100 check here for ya."

Andy's eyes widened a bit.

"Really?"

"Yeah. I mean, yeah, it's weird to go out and visit some place that labels itself a 'porn' site, but, dude, this is just a sign of good faith. If you get creeped out or just don't want to do anything, you can still take the money with you; it's not a big deal."

Andy's mood brightened. He got the details and, lacking anything better to do, locked his room, got to his car, and began driving to ROFL, Inc.

———

When Andy walked into the address he was given, he was impressed. Taking up the first floor of a fairly sizable building in the business district downtown, ROFL was quite the professional operation. There was even a desk up front with a secretary. Red pantsuit and tight brown hair in a bun, this female clerk wasn't too bad on the eyes. Andy walked up to the desk, flips slapping behind him.

"Um, hi – I'm here for a meeting with Mike?"

"Down the hall on the left, first door on the right." She pointed down the hall and smiled at him. Andy reactively smiled back, feeling a bit more at ease. Mike wasn't lying: this was the real deal. Andy made his way into Mike's office. Mike seemed like a late-20s everyman – a charismatic, simple guy who had an honest face and spoke in a direct manner.

"Andy?"

"Um, yeah, that's me."

"Great! I'm Mike!" The two shook hands. "Please, sit down." Andy pulled up a chair as Mike reclined behind his desk. Mike reached into his desk and pulled out an envelope. He tossed it across his desk to Andy.

"And there's your check for $100."

"Already?"

"Andy, I'm a man of my word. If you wind up working here, I want you do understand that."

"So," Andy started, "what is it you guys do?"

"Tickling," said Mike quite bluntly. "Just… tickling."

"… is there an audience for that?"

"Oh boy!" chortled Mike. "You have no idea good sir. Indeed, male tickling is a huge, huge market. To see a masculine collegiate type like yourself dissolve into fits of laughter – it's the crumpling of the male ego on a physical scale, and, well, that's pretty damn hard to resist. It's sexy, and, yes, people pay a lot to see it."

"So, what you're saying is… I would be paid for a video of another guy tickling me?"

"It's not that simple." Andy looked confused, but Mike continued onward: "Andy, follow me."

Mike lead Andy to a large, almost metallic room. It was dark and cold, the walls a dull, damp gray. In the middle was a table with padded straps, perfect for restraining someone. A little bit above, there was a booth with a large glass panel, not too dissimilar from a producer's booth in a recording studio. Mike walked around, demonstrating.

"This is where all the action happens. Basically, ROFL is a website, and subscribers come to us in order to see boys get tickled. They're strapped to this table and, for 60 straight minutes, are tickled pretty relentlessly. Some subscribers pay just to watch, while others pay even more to participate."

"What do you mean, 'participate'?"

Mike stopped for a second, thinking of how to respond. "Andy, sit down on the table – let me show you."

"Hey, you're not strapping me down to anything yet."

"Oh no no – this is just a demonstration. I'll lightly restrain your ankles and that's it – you can undo them at any time. OK?"

Andy stared at Mike questioningly.

"I'm a man of my word, remember?"

"Alright," said Andy. He slid off his flips and sat at the center of the table, soon swinging his lightly-hairy legs around just so that his legs were positioned where the ankle-straps were. Mike said "Hey – why don't you restrain your own ankles while I move up to the booth." Andy obliged.

From the booth, Mike spoke on the intercom: "You ready?"

"As I'll ever be, I guess" said the young victim. Mike, hard as he might, could barely contain his hardon, as – undoubtedly – Andy had the single best pair of feet he had ever seen. Yet Mike was a pro: he knew not to mix business with pleasure, and today, of all days, was all about business.

"Here we go" said Mike as he flipped on a switch.

Andy looked above and saw a giant set of lasers at the high ceiling above him. A green one lighted up and hovered about a foot away from his left foot. He watched closely as the green laser rest, immobile. Andy looked under the table to see if it was burning a hole in the floor – but no, it wasn't.

"OK, it's happening now…" warned Mike, ominously.

The laser slowly inched its way towards Andy's foot, then lightly pressed on his heel. It felt like… a finger. A soft – but direct – finger. It stayed on his heel for a bit, then slowly moved to the ball of his foot and began moving around. It was tickling him.

Andy was giggling slightly, but tried his hardest to contain it. The laser inched around a bit more, moving slowly – ever slowly – across Andy's sole. Up to the middle portion. Licking the sides of his wide size 13 feet, and then up to the base of his toes. Andy couldn't contain it anymore, and laughter came pouring out of him like a faucet on full-blast. A few seconds passed before the laser inched its way to the space between Andy's big and first toes, and that's when he cried out "No more!!"

The laser stopped. Mike was seen leaving the booth and then came down to the main room. Andy was catching his breath as Mike entered, soon b-lining to the straps at Andy's feet and undoing them. "What'd you think?" Mike asked.

"That was intense, dude."

"Yeah – now imagine a dozen of those going at once."

Andy froze – yet, somehow, was intrigued.

The tour continued, Mike finding a water bottle for the one-minute victim, and soon the young men were touring the spa-facilities, the locker rooms, etc. At one point Mike showed Andy the nano-fiber technology that allowed subscribers to slowly "burn" the clothes that a model was wearing. When asked about underwear and the likes, Mike explained the password system that had been set up in place. Finally, the boys returned to Mike's office. They sat down in the original positions.

"So," Andy started, "I don't mean to be a snob or anything, but I gotta ask…"

"Money."

"Right."

"Well, it's pretty simple, Andy. If you do one 60-minute session, you get $1000. In the form of a check. Payable on the spot."

Andy's jaw just about dropped on the floor. "Just… just for guys to tickle me for an hour?"

"Think you're man enough?"

Andy's mind just stopped right there. *Man enough?*, he thought. Of *course* he was man enough. But he wasn't going to let his ticklishness stand in the way of him losing a spot on the wrestling team or anything else like that. He was going to use it as a way to prove his strength – by standing up to it… just not now.

"Well Mike," started Andy, "I gotta say – that's a pretty sweet deal you're putting in front of me. But, I got to give it some time."

Mike nodded. "Totally understandable. Well, if you ever want to start, just give me a call, and we can fit you in within an hour. You know where we are, and" – extending his hand – "it's a pleasure to meet you."

"Likewise."

Andy made his way out the office, out the building, and back to his car. He felt pretty good about things right now, then thought of the $100 check he had pocketed. He was going to deposit it tomorrow, but, to be honest, he felt kind of guilty for just taking money from this guy, especially given how nice he was. Yet, he didn't let such a thought weigh him down – he was in a good mood for the first time in a while.

———

Andy felt like shit. He was nearing tears of rage. He couldn't believe it.

"But why?!" he shouted into his phone.

"Well," cooed Sophie, "I just need to move on. I'm sorry – it's nothing against you – I just, well, I just need to figure some stuff out with my life."

"That's not even a reason!" fumed Andy. "You slept with someone, I know it! Just tell me!"

"Listen, Andy…"

"Don't LISTEN ANDY me! What is it? What's causing you to leave me?"

"Listen, Andy, I am not up for being yelled at right now. I'll call you back when you're ready to talk like a real man."

The last words stung the most – even more than the click that followed it. Andy was enraged. He threw his pillow against a wall and pounded on his mattress as hard as he could. "Not man enough" he reiterated. He couldn't believe Sophie just broke up with him over the phone. Probably sleeping with some other guy back home. This wasn't even possible in Andy's universe. No matter how furiously he paced, no matter how hard he punched his mattress, the rage wasn't going away. That was the worst part of it all. Not man enough. He was the manliest man he knew – what a bullshit excuse that was. Andy wanted to go out there right now and punch the guy she was sleeping with just to prove the exact opposite to her. It wasn't flawless logic, but, hell, it worked for him.

Then he saw the number. That slip of paper. Perhaps he was a little off-kilter, but Andy… no, he couldn't. Could he? He looked around the room, thought of all his friends that he'd call and complain to – no, he needed something physical… and he needed it now.

Ringing. "Hey there, this is Mike."

"Mike! It's Andy! I'm coming in!"

"Um, Andy… from two weeks ago – right! Hi! You're… coming in?"

"Right the fuck now."

"Are you OK, man?"

"Just have your nano-stuff ready in 20 minutes. I want this to happen now."

Andy got in his car and drove furiously, his sneakered foot pressing so hard against the accelerator it was almost becoming one with it. Nothing was making this rage go away. Fuck Sophie. She had to be cheating on him – that was the only possible excuse. As Andy drove into the ROFL parking lot with the night sky hanging overhead, he knew this was, really, the last place he could go to try and deflate his rage.

Andy walked in, stormed past the secretary, and went right into Mike's office, catching him a bit by surprise.

"Andy, you're…"

"C'mon – let's suit me up!"

Mike's face went quiet – something was wrong… but he wasn't about to deny this model what he wanted. "Follow me" he said, leading to the locker room.

Within 20 minutes, the now sock-footed, nano-fabric-wearing Andy was strapped into the table in the giant laser room. Mike finished adjusting the final wrist-strap, when he began explaining the sensor screen up in the booth to him: "So, basically Andy, there's this video screen that shows your body. By itself, everyone can get to you, declothe you and tickle you. If I put my hands over your feet, however, the lasers can't touch them – the touch screen detects that my hands are there protecting you. Even if you give them your pants and boxers passwords, I can still protect you if…"

"Listen!" shouted the restrained Andy. "I just want to feel something right now. Anything. So take the night off, and let me have the next hour to myself in front of the world. I'm a man, OK – I don't need protection from anything."

Mike, flabbergasted, simply shrugged. "Alright – it's your session."

With that, Mike went up to the booth and started the five-minute countdown, noting the subscriber base piling in online to catch a glimpse of the new meat. Below, Andy sat shaking his head in defiance, wondering what the hell he was doing but still unable to shake Sophie's betrayal from his mind. Such bitterness and rage – he just wanted to feel something. No matter what.

The clock counted down, and hit zero – the lights dimmed.

And nothing happened.

Andy looked around, and saw all the lasers overhead (or at least the ones he could make out) were warmed and charged... but nothing was happening. He sat there for 10 seconds... 20... and nothing. He was just strapped down to a table dressed in silky fabric and his ankle socks. Well this sucks, he thought. Then, a red laser appeared. Right next to his waist. It slowly, surely, moved to the bottom of his shirt... and as it dragged across his shirt, it began dissolving it. Andy looked in amazement – this was kind of cool, actually. Another red laser appeared and began working on his left sleeve. With his hands bound to the table, Andy was basically spread-eagle and unable to move. Yet he found this clothes-dissolution technology fascinating. More red lasers appeared, and began working.

After about 10 minutes, his nano-shirt was mostly scraps, but after Andy's boredom set in 5 minutes into the process, all he could think back to was Sophie. Then a green laser appeared.

It was on the edge of his nano-pants, but since he divulged no password, his pants were unaffected. Then, the green laser moved slightly up, and touched the exposed skin right beneath his belly button. It kind of... tickled. Then it moved up a bit more, moving around his stomach hairs a bit. Andy giggled a bit, but thought not much of it... until the laser found the inside of his belly button.

Suddenly, it felt as if some warm, flexible finger had found its way into his belly button and began worming its way around there. The giggles began coming up in Andy's body, and, as hard as he tried, he just couldn't repress that smile anymore. It's almost as if the laser was hunting for tickles, and the biggest deposit was right there in his belly button. The giggling was turning into short, stuttered laughter... and soon he just burst, and began laughing. Then, another green laser appeared, and it was focusing on Andy's right armpit. He tried to drag his body to the left... but his bonds kept him motionless. Another pair of green lasers appeared, this time focused on his socks, slowly forcing those fleeting bits of cotton off of Andy's massive, delicious soles. Then another green appeared on his nipple. Andy began laughing a bit more. No, a lot more. His body was slowly going against his will, shaking and vibrating without his consent. Indeed, Andy was being tickle-tortured.

Twenty minutes in, Andy cried out "SOPHIE!" Not because he was thinking about her... but because that was the password for his pants. As soon as he said it, red lasers began appearing on the cuffs of his pantlegs, slowly dissolving them all while Andy dissolved into a puddle of uncontrollable laughter. His arms flexed and strained against his bonds, but it was useless – he wasn't going anywhere, and he had to accept his ticklish fate. Sophie's betrayal wasn't in Andy's mind anywhere – just the continual inescapable thought of tickling and being tickled. It was too much for him. He was going crazy, sweat pouring out of every pore of his body. Hell, he could even feel the green lasers in his armpit actually move the sweat around. Christ, this was potent stuff. He glanced down at his legs, his bared feet tops now staring at him as his toes wiggled uncontrollably. One green laser was focused entirely on the space between his toes, and it was driving him batty, Andy now worried he was about to choke on his own spit it was that intense. As the red lasers slowly began working their way up to his kneecaps, green lasers followed right behind them, stimulating him in a way he hadn't ever known before...

... in fact, Andy thought he was getting a bit of a hardon, which he thought was impossible. All of these slightly warm lasers were caressing him. Yes, guys all over the world were caressing that fine, masculine body of his, using his rippling flesh as a canvas in which to paint a tickle masterpiece. Some lasers were erratic, others were slow and gradual, but they all had one purpose – to make him suffer. Somehow, being at the whims, the lusts, the desires of so many guys… it was turning him on, which would concern Andy more were he not being tickled on his neck by two more lasers. This was becoming too much.

Five minutes were left, and, finally, his pants were dissolved. He was now just down to his nano-boxers and the green lasers were having a field day on his inner thighs. Andy couldn't recall the last time he had been touched there, but it tickled like hell. Not just tickling either – erotic tickling. His waist was thrusting as much as it could to get away from the lasers, but most of his energy was still being used by his toes, splaying and contracting wildly to get away from the guys who were tickling his toes for the past ten minutes virtually non-stop. It was official, there was now a hardon brewing in those nano-boxers, and all the thrusting in the world wasn't helping him. Now even more lasers were focused on him, and – with that – a strange feeling washed over the boy… he suddenly, inexplicably, felt wanted. All of these guys wanted him to suffer, yes, but that's 'cos he was hot, and ticklish, and fun to tickle. Andy, in his fever-addled brain, felt needed and important for the first time in a long time. Suddenly, his ticklish anguish turned into euphoria. He wanted to overcome his preconceptions about what's straight and what's gay, and, in fact, wanted the guys out there to discover his boxers password. He garnered just enough breath the shout it… when the system shut down. The hour was up, and now Andy lay on the table, sweating, mostly naked, and horny as all hell. It wasn't long before Mike was untying him.

––––––––––

"So what'd you think?" asked Mike, massaging the massive feet of the new model in the locker room.

Andy, still sweating, mulled his answer carefully, as his brain was still trying to digest the experience he had just had. Andy glanced at Mike and said "Well… it was good. Yeah, I didn't mind it at all."

Mike smiled, working on the base of the toes hard enough to relax but not hard enough to tickle. He placed Andy's massive foot down on the bench and asked the only question he could ask: "So… are we going to see you again?"

Andy, his mind awash with all the details Mike had told him about generating the most paying users at a single time (50,000), thought that, yeah, he could do this again for another thousand. He grinned, glanced at Mike, and said "Yeah… and real soon, too."

THE LICKLE

The sequel to "The Ad". *Oh yeah.*

"Dude, what a rush!"

Andy, the confident, muscular college jock who was now on his second year of being on the wrestling team, was walking down the halls to the ROFL locker rooms, proudly wearing nothing but his nano-boxers and feeling oddly energized, despite the fact that his body was positively caked in sweat. Right behind him was Mike, towel and Gatorade in hand, giving casual encouragement to his young star.

"How'd we do tonight, Mike? I felt good about this one." asked Andy.

"Well," said Mike, glancing down at a clipboard, "your star turns are doing gangbuster business now. We had… shit, we had 200,000 viewers tonight, man!"

Andy stood at his locker, casually removing his nano-boxers before slipping into the hot-tub which Mike had installed for the "post-tickle relaxation" of his models. Mike looked around, amused: at least four other handsome collegiate models were walking around in various states of dress, all either coming back from being tickled or getting ready to be. Truly, ROFL, Inc. was growing into its own entity: it was now the #1 male tickle site in the world, as fans were willing to pay top dollar just to have Mike's patented nano-laser technology tickle the living hell out of writing, muscled young men. Even though working the screens each session was exhausting work, he couldn't help but be turned on by it – simply because he was living out his ultimate sexual fantasy every day. He turned it into a business – nay, an empire…

And here, in the bubbling pool below him, sat Andy, the site's most popular model. Though ROFL had caught the modeling attention of many gay young men – many who subscribed to the emo culture, oddly – Andy was, and still is, the only straight model who worked for the company, and, incidentally, the most popular by far. The 200,000 people who just watched him tonight was the icing on a cake that's been slowly baking for some time: over the months, Andy – probably due to his straightboy reactions alone – was outdrawing any other model 2-to-1. He talked back to the users who egged him on, and seemed to try and deny his ticklish nature as much as he could, often grimacing and biting his teeth during the first 5 minutes of any given session. Over time, people couldn't get enough of Andy, and Andy couldn't get enough of tickling: it was turning into quite the adrenaline rush for him.

Yet Mike didn't have time to think about that now. Andy got back out of the hottub, put on his running shorts and T-shirt, slipped on his worn leather flip-flops, and opened his hand as Mike handed the boy a $6000 check. For an hour of work a night, Andy was getting paid quite, quite nicely. Mike wished him adieu, and with that, these two unlikely business partners ended yet another spectacularly profitable night.

It was 9PM by the time that Andy left the ROFL offices, and drove his car back to campus. The moon was out, the clouds lightly hazy, the air warm: all of this made for one happy Andy. He began walking back to his dorm room and heard his flips echo as they slapped against his meaty soles across the quad. He got out his keys, almost made it to the door, when suddenly he heard a voice behind him.

"Andy?"

The voice was unfamiliar. Andy turned around and saw… a frosh standing there. Short, messy blonde hair, glasses, ripped blue jeans and flips. Also wearing a plain white T-shirt as well – just like Andy. As he examined the new campus creature, Andy's eyebrow arched.

"Um, can I help you?"

"Hey man, I… man, I'm sorry, I don't really know how to say this…"

"Just say it man" said Andy, rather non-chalantly.

"Well… I tickled you tonight."

Andy's eyes burst wide open. This was complete news to him.

"You what?"

"Well," started the frosh, "I've just had this foot fetish for as long as I can remember. For guys' feet, of course. I don't even know where it came from. Well, I just gradually became so obsessed with them that I became obsessed with what I could do them, and, well, when I saw one of your tickle sessions on ROFL last year I… well, that's when I really knew who I was."

"Wait… what?" chortled Andy.

"I dunno, it's hard to explain. When I saw you get tickled, there was just something about it, just something… really, really cool. It all made sense, somehow. Especially your feet man. I mean, even now…" The frosh glanced down briefly at Andy's toes in his flips, "I just can't help but be a little overwhelmed. I can't tell you how badly I want to worship them."

"Worship them?"

"Yeah, you know – sucking on your toes and whatnot."

Both stood there for a moment, in silence. A small breeze swept through the space between them.

Andy started: "What's your name?"

"Caleb."

Andy snickered. "Well, Caleb – anything's worth doing once, right?"

Andy led the young lad in, up to his single on the third floor of his dorm. The common room was occupied by jocks watching *SportsCenter* or studying, some with girlfriends nearby. Andy gave his casual "what's up" to the guys and led Caleb into his own room. Caleb walked in, only to find Andy having set up a bit of a shrine to himself: wrestling trophies, medals, an old basketball jersey from high school. Andy was always proud of his accomplishments, and wanted others to know it. Caleb was somewhat awe-struck by the surroundings, at least until Andy's door clicked and locked behind him. Andy then jumped up on his bed, his legs hanging over and flips dangling from between his toes.

"So," started Andy, "you an English major?"

"Um, yeah. Well, not officially yet, but that's what I'm going to do…. how'd you guess?"

"I dunno," Andy smirked. "Just had a hunch."

"I see," said Caleb, smiling slightly.

"So how does this work?"

"Well," started Caleb in a slightly more authoritative tone, "why don't you lie on your bed length-wise, like a normal person?"

"Heh, OK" said Andy. His head was now on his pillow, his feet near the foot of his bed – like a normal person. Caleb swiftly moved to where his feet were, placed his hands right on the soles of Andy's flips, and took a deep, considered breath.

"You ready?" Caleb asked.

"Go crazy, dude."

Caleb's smile grew much wider.

The hands slowly slid the flips off of Andy's left foot, then his right, almost as if he was enjoying the feeling of removing the leathery beasts from Andy's sensitive skin. Caleb took a deep inhale from the spots where Andy's toes had left sweat-stains. He was totally enjoying it. The flops both clunked to the floor. Andy stopped looking at Caleb and began looking at the ceiling, just enjoying whatever was about to happen to him.

Caleb's nimble fingers went up and began slowly, slowly massaging Andy's soles. They reminded Andy a lot of Mike's foot massages. They were relaxing. Then – Andy felt it. His big toe on his left foot enter Caleb's eager, hungry mouth. The toe was wrapped in a warm, wet place, that was oddly comforting. Caleb's mouth slowly went up the toe and down, slowly again, almost imitating a blowjob. Caleb's anxious tongue began repeating this with other toes, and Andy... wasn't sure what to feel. Whatever it was, it sure as hell felt good though. Almost too good. Then Caleb's tongue began slowly entering the space between Andy's toes, forcing them apart with Caleb's meaty, wet mouthworm. Had Andy looked, he'd see Caleb's hardon positively raging through his jeans. Then Andy noticed… he was hard too.

His cock was very, very erect. All this toe-sucking and sole-licking was driving Andy wild. The sole-licking was the worst part, as it tickled like hell – but it in a teasing, sensual way. Andy was truly getting off on this. Caleb began trying to fit all five of Andy's right toes in his mouth at once, as if he was consuming Andy whole. Andy couldn't help it anymore: almost subconsciously, he began teasing his own cockhead through his shorts fabric. The more he teased himself, the lustier Caleb was getting, and it wasn't too long before both men climaxed. The surprising thing: Andy climaxed bigger, flexing his toes while they were still firmly within Caleb's mouth, the tongue tickling his toe pads as his cock was shooting load after load. Andy felt like he was in heaven.

———————

Hours later, after Andy had shown Caleb out, Andy lied in his room, barefoot and in boxer shorts, mulling the experience over and over in his head. He couldn't believe how much he enjoyed it. It was incredible. You're damn right he was going to have it again. But… well, maybe this means that Andy was meant for more things. He was beyond where he was when he was a Freshman – maybe it was truly time for him to start anew. He contemplated about all the dozens upon dozens of tickle sessions he had done for Mike at ROFL. He thought maybe it was time – maybe it was time for him to go out while he was still on top. In fact, there was no maybe about it – it was definitely his time. Andy went to his laptop, sent an e-mail to Mike saying that his scheduled session on Friday would be his last one.

Andy was awoken by his cell phone the next morning. It was Mike.

"Hello?"

"What do you mean it's your last session, man?"

"I dunno, Mike. I just… I just feel open to a lot more things now. I need to move on – I'm almost graduated, man!"

"But dude – you still got most of a year left."

"I know, I know. I just… you can't keep doing something if you don't feel it, ya know? I mean, I'm on top of my game right now, so why not quit while I'm ahead?"

There was a pause on the other line.

"You're right, Andy" started Mike. "Just know that I've really, really enjoyed your time here."

"Slow down, dude! I still got another session left!"

"I know, I know" said Mike, obviously disappointed.

Andy thought for a second. This was Mike afterall – the guy who may very well have paid for his entire college education.

"How about this, Mike? It can be a two-hour session. And… I promise this time, if they get me, I'll give up the underwear password."

Mike's heart skipped two beats – you could practically hear it on the other end.

"That's… that's great, Andy! I mean… wow. Really?"

"I figure I owe ya one. Oh, and I bet you can probably charge whatever you want this time around."

"You're right…"

"So I'll see you Friday then?"

"Absolutely."

"Later, man."

Andy hung up the phone. He checked the ROFL site an hour later. "Andy's last session" it proclaimed. "$500 a pop!" Andy's eyes widened. He was worth that much? He thought about the paycheck he'd receive right after… and yes, he was worth that much. Andy then logged into Facebook, quite happy with his worth to the world. Caleb submitted a Friend Request. Had it been any other night, Andy would've said no, but being on the celebrity high he was on, he accepted. Yes, this really was a new life for him.

———————

As Andy entered the ROFL offices that Friday, models would stop in the hallways and applaud him, pat him on the back. Andy didn't realize it, but many of the guys who were working as tickle victims on the site were working there because of Andy's early, early vids. When Andy walked into the locker room, at least two dozen models were there – some Andy hadn't even seen for months, even – gathered around and cheering for him. "BEST LAST TICKLE" it even said on a banner suspended above. Andy blushed with gratitude. Soon, the crowd of guys opened up to show Mike right in front of Andy's locker, a cake on a small table right there. "BEST MODEL EVER" it said on the cake. Andy put his finger in it to taste a sample. "Chocolate? That's my favorite, Mike! How did you know?" Mike smiled sheepishly: "'cos you told me once."

As the people cleared out and Andy got dressed, Andy thought about all of the great memories he had here, and thought that maybe this place meant more to him than he thought. Yet it was no time to get nostalgic: he had one helluva tickle session to through. As he was dressing into nano-fibers, Mike stood in the doorway leading out to the hallway, just as he always did. Andy spoke up: "so how many people we got subscribed tonight?"

"You don't want to know, man."

"Oh, c'mon Mike. Just tell me."

"How does 300,000 sound?"

Andy froze.

"I thought that 200,000 was your best number."

"It was, Andy. Apparently some people have been talking, and suddenly we have 100,000 more subscribers."

"But we sure as hell don't have 300,000 lasers."

"Oh I know – I narrowed it down to the 10 strongest lasers, and then had a raffle amidst all the subscribers. There were some very lucky subscribers tonight."

"Heh, sweet."

Mike walked over a bit.

"Hey Andy?"

"What's up?"

"Do you mind if the other models watch from the booth tonight?"

"Oh dude – I'd love it if they watched me get tickled to death." Andy realized this thought intrigued him as he said it – maybe there was a kinkier side to him than he thought.

Soon, nano-socks on and everything, Mike walked Andy down the hall to the Tickle Room for one last go. Both guys were excited. They were going to make history. As soon as Andy walked into the room itself, the online crowd began cheering. Andy could hear the voices pumping through the speakers. He felt like Russell Crowe in Gladiator, all these people cheering for him in his kinky coliseum. He raised his arms, expecting more cheers. He got it.

Soon, Mike strapped him down to the table, just as always. Mike went up to the booth, and Andy glanced up: there was a sea of familiar faces up there, watching their star take his final send-off. Andy would've saluted them if he could, but he was strapped down to the table pretty tight – as always.

The clock began. 30 seconds until tickle.

The memories began flooding back. Suddenly Andy was getting nostalgic. 20 seconds. He really was going to miss this place. Truly. 10 seconds. 9. 8. 7. 6. 5. 4.…

And then everything stopped.

The lasers started chugging, the lights dimmed. There was a power surge, and the equipment wasn't handling it well. Andy looked up at the booth, and through the glimmers of light, he could see Mike panicking. A few minutes passed. Nothing happened.

Then, finally, Mike got onto the loudspeaker.

"Hey Andy – the lasers aren't working… so we're going to try something."

Andy was confused. Then he saw the door to the room open, and ten of his model friends came into the room, each of them wearing earpieces. Wait a second, Andy thought, if there were 10 subscribers that still needed tickle play, and 300,000 subscribers waiting for his every move, then… oh no.

Andy was in a room of horny tickle laser substitutes.

"Let's begin," started one.

Andy let out a bellowing scream, but it was too late to stop anything now.

The models' wiggling fingers slowly encroached in on him, and Andy – perhaps being at human hands instead of robot ones – had never felt more helpless in his life. His midsection tried jerking and twisting to escape, but it was too late. The first too-long set of fingernails descended on the soft, silk-like nanofabric right above his stomach, and Andy giggled. Then there hands on his pits, arms, ribs, thighs, and feet. Especially the feet. Andy couldn't stop giggling: he began fully laughing now. Shit, he thought. This was terrible. The 10 selected ticklers were all feeding Andy with devious tickle thoughts, and each of these surrogates was carrying it out – with relish. Suddenly, the whole "passwords" thing was irrelevant: Andy knew that the second that his smooth nano-socks slipped right off. His big, meaty jock feet sat there exposed to the world, and the fingernails were thoroughly enjoying the experience.

One hand was swiping the ball of his foot, another feeling his nipples through the nanofabric, another teasing his neck, all making him feel even more defenseless. The worst part? These hands weren't stopping. The lasers always had a consistent tickle speed, but these hands seemed to be getting hungrier as they kept on tickling his sensitive little body. Andy would've pleaded to stop, but all that emerged was laughter. Completely uncontrollable laughter.

By the time both his nanoshirt and nanopants were gone, Andy looked up at the big clock in the room. Only 20 minutes had passed. He wasn't sure how much longer he could endure the tickling. Then it stopped. The models all stopped tickling him. One of the models – bleach-blonde short hair – was telling the others about something the guy in his earpiece was saying. Then, the model actually removed the earpiece and put it up to Andy's ear, all while his sweaty chest heaved desperate buckets of air. The voice in the earpiece spoke.

"Hey there, Andy."

Andy froze for a second. "CALEB?!"

"You ready for this?"

"Wh-what?"

The model placed the earpiece back in his own ear. The model then spoke loudly: "So, according to this guy, Andy is most ticklish when he's being licked…"

Andy thought he was out of energy until he heard that sentence: now he was rocking his bonds as hard as he could, trying to break free, but it was no use: he was going to be "lickled"…

It started with the toes. One models' tongue began quickly darting between the toes of his left foot… then his right. Another tongue began circling his nipple. Yet another was painting his inner-thigh with saliva. Yet the two guys who were at his armpits: those tongues began slowly, slowly moving over his cavernous arm-interiors, almost savoring his pit-hair and sweaty buildup. It was like leading a horse to a salt-lick: these 10 tongues just couldn't get enough of Andy. Suddenly, Andy was the most-wanted man in the world. Over 100,000 subscribers had already came at the very sight of it – something that Andy would never know.

The foot tongues were going crazy, up and down the soles, taking a particular interest in the tops of his feet, and truly, truly not stopping. The nipple tongues had moved to his neck, the armpit tongues weren't letting up, and a new one was finding every crevice to be found in his belly-button. Yet the two tongues on his thighs were having the most fun: they were moving up to his nano-briefs, and they began circling the edge of the nano fabric between each leg hole. Andy, lost in lusty laughter and frustration, was showing a hardon so badly. Then, in one swoop, the nanoboxers were ripped off. At least five tongues jumped right to his cock's needs. Five tongues, almost in a starfish formation, began painting the cock up and down. Two tongues went down while two others went up, another licking the space right underneath his balls. The tongues at his feet – now completely moist with saliva – were sucking his big toes quite hard. Andy didn't have any choice: he shot the load to beat all loads. His jizz flew everywhere.

The tongues stopped briefly… then went right back at it. It's as if they purposely extracted the seed from the aching, ticklish jock boy – and just like the tickle hands before – they wanted more. Andy glanced up at the clock… and he was only 40 minutes into his 120 minute session. Then, as one tongue made a giant sweep across his sole, Andy realized: he was more sensitive than he was before. He screamed again, but the scream turned into desperate, pleading laughter moments later. The most powerful wrestler in college was turned into a horny mass of tickleflesh, and there was nothing – nothing – he could do about it.

Andy walked into his room. Tears were caked on his cheeks from the goodbyes, and there was some bits of cake left between his toes from what happened after his historic session. Andy sat at his desk with a $50,000 check in his hands. He thought of how he would never go back there. He thought of all the things he missed about his fun routine. He missed all of it already.

He logged into Facebook. He found Caleb's profile. Almost without thinking, Andy typed a private message to Caleb.

"Next session: where/when?"

Andy got a reply within 30 seconds.

THE MASTER

It had been awhile since I read either "Foot Club" or "Affluent", but as time went on, people gradually began showing a strong desire to see sequels to each of these stories tackled individually. In rereading them, however, I discovered that there was absolutely no reason whatsoever that Todd and Kyle couldn't be living on the same campus, possibly just unaware of each other's existence. As such, the resulting story was a continuation of both their tales, intersecting with the introduction of a brand new character, one who, as you will discover, still has many more erotic adventures ahead of him...

This couldn't be happening.

No, no – there is no way that this could be happening. There the boys were, stripped to their boxers and tied to each other on the hotel bed, stomach-to-stomach. Their hands were wrapped around the other's ribcage, like an awkward-yet-effective hug. Neither could move except for their hands, the guys' bared ankles trapped in an elaborate web of zip-ties. The young 20-somethings looked in each other's eyes and could see that they were experiencing the same feeling: a mixture of excitement and undeniable mortal terror. The hotel wall lamp was all that was lighting their sweat-drenched bodies, and that's exactly how The Master liked it. "OK, boys," the Master started, "one of you is going to be my Tickle Toy for the evening. But I want to see which one wants it more – therefore, you are going to tickle each other into submission. The first one to relent is going to be put in a world of – heh – delights…" The Master snickered. "So it's tickle or be tickled, young squires. Any questions?"

Todd spoke up and said "Yeah…", then turning to his collegiate tickle counterpart (whose fingers were starting to softly circle the area just below Todd's pits). "What's your name?" The other boy laughed a bit: "Kyle."

"Enough of the small talk!" shouted The Master. "Now… BEGIN!"

———————

Two months had passed since Todd had been initiated into Foot Club, and he was already the Club's rising star. After his first night of ticklish humiliation, Todd knew he was hooked for life. All the Facebook pics and MySpace posts by the Club's other members had made Todd into something of a reluctant campus celebrity. Though the concept of "Foot Club" was floated around discussions of various cliques, very few dare ask what all those pictures of Todd sucking frat toes was all about. Just one week afterwards, the frat members who started the Club were soon calling up Todd – not for a worship session, but to see a movie, to go to a campus party, etc. The sheer intensity of his first ordeal would've broken any soul, but Todd's passion for worship was even stronger, and through it, he preserved. No other initiation in the history of the college was as intense: Todd had become something of a legend.

Two weeks later, Todd received a Facebook message from a kid named Jason who, Todd later found out, sat two rows behind him in his Philosophy of Art class. Jason sent a message of admiration: not only praising Todd's audacity to endure what (at least through the Facebook pics) appeared to be a tumultuous tickle experience, but also giving Todd an unusual compliment – that his feet looked real good in flip-flops. Even as text on a screen, Todd felt that Jason's message was shy, like words whispered out at a loud party. The next day, right as the bell ended in that same class, Todd winked at Zach as he walked out but outstretched his arm to stop Jason right there in his tracks.

"Hey dude" started Todd, speaking as a much more confident individual than he was before he came to this school.

"Oh, hey there Todd" stammered Jason, his shoulder-length locks of hair slightly obscuring his face.

"So, I got your message."

"Oh yeah… sorry, that was just kind of a… in the moment kind of thing…"

"Dude, it's OK. I've got the same fetish, man."

A small smile broke out on Jason's face. Todd then did something entirely pompous and self-serving… but something he'd been wanting to try for awhile. He placed his hand right at the back of Jason's head and said "Go ahead, look."

It took Jason a second to figure it out, but Todd's hand slowly directed Jason's gaze down upon Todd's flip-flopped feet. The toes wiggled a bit in recognition, but Jason simply sat there, mouth agape. He stood like this for several seconds, the classroom now empty as people staggered to lunch.

"I… I feel kind of guilty for looking." Jason was almost shivering as he said it.

"It's OK, Jason – I like the attention." Jason's smile emerged again. Todd then leaned over and whispered something in his ear:

"Tell me… what do you want to do them?"

Jason took a second, and carefully considered his next words: "I would love to… worship your feet."

Todd grinned. "Then follow me."

Todd opened the door to his room and let Jason enter first. Todd followed and then locked the door behind him. Jason – decked out in long jeans and black tennis shoes – took a moment to absorb the room in. Jason was obviously nervous, but he had an excitement about him… as if stunned he had made it this far, all that much closer to making his private fantasies a reality. Jason finally was able to indulge in a bit of small talk:

"So, um, you live alone?"

"No, man. I live with a guy named Doug. Kinda bearded, in a lot of plays, etcetera. Know him?"

"I think I had Beginning Acting with him…"

"Yeah, real cool guy." Todd sat at his computer chair and propped his still-sandaled feet up on his desk. Jason caught himself staring again.

"So, is Doug... does he know about your fetish?"

Todd grimaced a little. "Um, well... that's not important now. The important thing is simply this – how badly do you want my feet?"

Jason was stunned by the abruptness of the question "Well, I... a lot. I want them very badly."

"So, you'd be willing to go through a lot to get 'em, right?"

"Well, I guess I..."

"Tell me," said Todd in a slightly menacing tone "... are you ticklish, Jason?"

Todd recognized the look: the wide-eyed admission of defeat.

"Well, yes, but I hate being tickled, and I can't stand..."

"But do you hate it enough to be rewarded with feet at the end?" said Todd, interrupting.

Jason's face was blank. Was it worth it? Could he do it?

Ten minutes later, Jason was in no position to take back his own damning response: "I'd do anything for your feet, Jason!"

At present, a nice area of Todd's floor had been cleared. Jason was down to his boxers, laying hog-tied on the floor, face-down. His hands and feet were bound tight behind him... and oh, what feet they were. Size 9's that were soft and pink, sensitive to being in socks practically their entire life. Jason had been bound with white nylon rope that Todd bought during his first week at school (in hopes of packing), and the young freshman boy was completely immobile. Todd sat next to the boy with his legs outstretched, Jason's knees right next to his crotch, leaving Todd's legs to cradle Jason's bound body, Todd's barefeet only inches away from Jason's face on either side. Jason could already smell them, despite the toes being more than six inches away from his nose. Jason was in ecstasy. He tried to turn and look at the face of his captor behind him, but could only wrangle a side glance:

"So, how long do I have to endure?"

Todd flashed a wicked grin: "Until I'm happy."

With Jason's outflexed, bound toes facing the ceiling (and at chin-level), Todd decided to have a little fun with his prey. First, he moved his nose down to Jason's toes, and inhaled a bit. What a joyous scent. Then, he flickered his tongue right at the base of those toes, right on the pads of the soles. Jason already began to giggle. Oh, this was going to be fun. Without warning, Todd began dragging his fingernails slowly across Jason's feet, from heel to toe-base, and all he could hear was the boy yelp and yelp and yelp. If Todd could've seen Jason's face from his position, he would've seen it twist and distort into a fun-house mirror menagerie of smiles. Some tried to hold back the laughter, while others just gave in. When Jason closed his eyes, it seemed to help hold back the laughter a bit, but anytime he opened them, he saw Todd's big bared soles on either side of him, flexing and moving and driving him wild. Ten seconds into his tickle torture, and already Jason couldn't take anymore.

But this didn't stop Todd – he was too busy using his perfectly-trimmed nails to explore the tops of Jason's feet… then the sides of them… and then he spent a lot of time lightly dancing over his ankles. Oh, how Jason writhed. The body bouncing around between Todd's legs, like a blue jean lasso in which the young boy was ensnared. Unable to complete a coherent word, Jason just kept laughing and laughing, Todd now seeing what areas of Jason's feet yielded what kinds of desperate sounds, interspersing the tickling with frequent tongue explorations of the sensitive flesh between Jason's toes. Jason's boxers did little to prevent the freshman's expanding erection from grinding into the cheap rug beneath him, but, really, Jason's sense of time was completely gone, and he had little sense to adjust for such things.

Ten minutes had passed, and Todd was enthralled. Yet he saw tears of laughter dripping down Jason's face… and felt it was time to reward him. Todd inched his feet closer to Jason, who – as soon as he stopped laughing – began licking without being told to. Passionate, excited licking. All the energy that Jason had left from the tickling was being used to worship Todd's feet, an accomplishment made all the more amazing by the fact that Jason was completely immobile. Todd's fingertips lightly traced Jason's feet as he did this, but eventually the good feeling of having his feet worshipped was just too much for Todd, who went from a sitting position to a lying-down one, all with the hog-tied Jason still cradled between his legs. Todd's own rod began to respond in kind, and it wasn't long before he reached his own climax, his toes clenching in Jason's mouth just as how Todd's mouth clenched around Zach's toes all those many moons ago. It was incredible. As soon as Todd gathered the strength, he sat up and untied Jason, who almost collapsed entirely on the floor, splayed like an exhausted asterix on the ground. Todd heard Jason pant heavily.

"Enjoy it?" inquired Todd, his own brow sweating from the experience.

Jason could only squeeze this out between pants "Too much." Both smiled.

As Jason finished getting dressed a few minutes later, he asked "So, do you have a foot master that you serve?" Todd laughed confidently. "Not anymore."

Then, Doug walked in.

"What's up, Todd?" the bearded Scot beckoned.

"Hey there, Doug."

"Who's this?" Doug asked, pointing to Jason.

"Oh, just some…"

"I'm Jason."

Todd frowned a bit.

"Hello there, Jason," beamed Doug. "Nice to meet you."

Todd was growing anxious: "Jason, maybe you should go…"

"Why?" asked Doug, popping open his mini-fridge to grab a Heineken. "What's the rush?"

"Well, Jason just has a lot of…"

"What's wrong, Todd?" asked Jason. "Ashamed that I worshipped your feet?"

Todd stopped, blushing. Jason turned to look at Doug, whose eyebrow just arched in amusement.

"Oh, this is too good!" started Doug. Todd was almost yelling: "Jason, you should leave now, or…"

"Hey Jason" – Doug was speaking with a devilish grin – "want to see something cool?"

"Yeah!"

"No!" screamed Todd.

"Watch this!"

Doug handed Jason his beer, sat on the couch next to the wall of the room, and slowly began to untie his black Chuck Taylors. Slowly and deliberately. Todd's legs were braced as if he were about to sprint at any second, but he couldn't keep his eyes off of Doug's feet. Off came the Chuck's... slowly. Then the long, tall white socks... first the right one, leaving Doug's right foot bare and looking beautiful. Doug turned to Jason and said "would you care to do the other?" Jason smiled and eagerly – yet slowly – removed Doug's other long white sock. Now, Doug was barefoot. Doug propped his feet onto the yin-yang coffee table they purchased at the start of the year. Jason turned to Todd, who was trembling. "Go ahead," motioned Doug, "I know you want to." Todd buckled at the knees, and moved closer to Doug's feet. Without hesitation, he began sucking on Doug's toes with care and obedience. Doug relinquished his beer from Jason and took a swig. Jason stared in amazement.

"How... why is he doing this?"

"I dunno" said Doug, quite non-chalantly. "Dude just loves my feet."

"When did you find out?"

"The night I woke up with my toes in his mouth. He tries to be all confident and stuff, but, for whatever reason, my feet are the thing that makes him do whatever I want. I don't abuse my powers, but I just thought you should see this."

"I'm glad you're showing me" said Jason with a gluttonous grin. He turned to Doug and whispered "Hey, I might have a proposition for you..."

Todd tried to listen but couldn't make it out through the slurping sounds of his mouth against Doug's soles – he was absolutely helpless at the feet of the boy who he secretly loved. Doug never abused Todd's fetish, but he did find it amusing on occasion. If only Todd could hear what Doug and Jason were whispering to each other...

Two nights later, Todd was arriving home from a late-night fiction workshop (which, being college, was actually held at a nearby

Applebee's, the prof. paying for the whole meal). His new story just got torn to shreds, so Todd was just about ready to pass out. He found his keys, and turned the lock to his room… only to see the strangest sight he had ever seen. It was midnight, and the light from the hallway behind him was just enough to illuminate the vision in front of him: Doug's bared soles, floating.

They weren't floating of course, but the couch in the guys' room had been moved to the center of the room and turned sideways – Doug was merely propping his bared beauties up on the armrest so that when Todd walked in, it would be the first thing he saw. Todd sat aghast – the sight was hypnotic… yet somehow exactly what he needed. He took two steps into his room, when he heard Doug say "close the door". Todd obliged, plunging the room into semi-darkness (the moonlight still outlined Doug's perfect toes all too well). "Go ahead" said Doug, "just enjoy." Todd found the gesture odd… but who was he to resist? He set his backpack down, kneeled to the side of the couch, and, like an anxious puppy, began gently licking the greatest footflesh he had ever laid eyes on. As minutes past, Todd got more into it, encouraged by Doug's saying of "yes, good boy" over and over. Somehow, though, this seemed quite out of character for Doug. That's when Doug said the most out-of-character thing of all, though:

"Ya know, they're paying me a lot to set you up, Todd."

"Who is?"

"They are."

A black hood was put over Todd's eyes and a gag was stuffed into his mouth, with at least two pairs of arms (maybe three) all restraining him. As Todd pointlessly struggled while being carried out of the room, all Todd could hear was Doug saying "Enjoy your time with The Master…"

Another day, another list of appointments.

There Kyle stood, looking at the dry-erase board mounted on the door to the room he shared with Matt: "Foot Boy's Sign-Up Sheet". This was not something that Kyle initiated, instead something that Phil – his unofficial "Foot Master" – had started in the wake of that one time that Kyle sucked on Phil's unconscious toes without his permission. When Matt revealed Kyle's ticklish nature, Kyle had to pretty much give in to each and every whim that Phil had. The "Sign Up Sheet" was one of them, as any player on the swim team could sign up for an appointment to get their feet serviced. Kyle no longer had to pay his "clients", but Phil's rule was that they could tie him up and tickle them if he wanted (especially if he, you know, tried to wipe a name off of the sign-up sheet). Kyle dreaded it, but only in public. Secretly, he loved the fact that every day he got to indulge his favorite fetish of all time – as long as the guys didn't tickle him. Kyle hated being tickled, as that was his single, greatest weakness.

Really, Kyle hated being tickled because of Einstein.

E=MC2 and all that bullshit. He didn't like the transfer of energy ratios. He didn't like how a single index finger could wiggle a quarter of an inch on a patch of skin on his body (pick anywhere, really), and this would then cause his entire body to buck and convulse against his will. Really, it wasn't fair. At all. It was for this reason that he was happy to be rooming with Matt. Matt still had a rockin' swimmers body, but even though Matt was really Kyle's first worship experience (excepting Dylan, of course), Matt never forced Kyle to worship his succulent beauts... nor did he tickle him. He was somewhat like a protective older brother, occasionally telling Phil when enough was enough... even if he did go along with Phil's whims most of the time. In the end though, Kyle determined that he didn't really mind the tickling... as long as he got feet at the end of his day.

That night, Kyle thought of the recent session that he had with his friend Dylan when he visited him on campus, and just how flat-out intense it was, breaking all previous notions of what a foot worship session could accomplish. Really, that one experience proved to be what Kyle thought about alot, but it would soon be pushed out of his mind when Matt – shaved head and all – said the phrase that, oddly, would change Kyle's life:

"Dude, I think I found your twin."

"What?"

"Come here!" said Matt, gesturing towards his computer monitor.

What Kyle saw blew his mind.

Matt was on Facebook, looking at the pictures of a guy who appeared to be naked (the shots were carefully edited for content), bound on the floor of some fraternity house room while being tickled and forced to worship, literally, hundreds of horny frat toes. The shots were peppered with beer bottles and cans all over the place, but the guy sucking the toes… he seemed to be… enjoying it. Kyle was intrigued – not as much over the fact that here was someone who may actually share the same interest as him, but… he was also kind of handsome: short, dark hair, a respectable bod, etc. Then again, these could all be tricks his mind was playing: maybe it was a really, really humiliating ordeal that some frosh had to go through for initiation. Either-way, Kyle was intrigued.

"What's this?"

"I dunno" explained Matt, "I think it's one of those Foot Club meetings I hear about. Who knows – might be up your alley."

"I guess. What's this guy's name?"

"Um, let's see… Todd. Wait,… I think I know him. We took Math for Trees together."

"Math for Trees?"

"Yeah, it was like a crazy-easy math class. But yeah, nice guy. Guess he likes feet. And…" Matt clicked back to his profile, "looks like he lives in the building next to us."

"Larguinha Hall?"

"That's the one."

There was an awkward silence. Then, Matt said the most daring thing that Kyle had ever heard in his life: "Why don't you go see him?"

"Um… I wouldn't expect you to encourage me in that respect, Matt. I mean, I'm grateful and all, but…"

Matt stopped him. "Dude, it makes you happy. You should do what makes you happy, and it's even better if you could share it with someone. 'sides… I could use the place to myself for an night. I could, um, take care of some things…"

Kyle stared blankly. Then he got it.

"Oh."

"Yeah," said Matt. "It's like walking around with a loaded gun."

Kyle grinned. "It's OK man – you've let me indulge myself enough in here." Kyle slipped on some sneakers and was out the door before he knew it. The second the cool night air hit his skin though, Kyle realized that he had absolutely no idea what he was going to do if he saw this Todd guy.

The door to Larguinha Hall was propped open (sounded like a kegger was transpiring on the second floor), so Kyle just had to stroll in. He went up to the third floor, where the Facebook page said Todd was, but Kyle never got a room number. He was hoping some of the guys would at least have the courtesy to put their names on at least one of the doors. First door: blank. Second door: there was a mirror for some reason. Third door… suddenly burst open.

Kyle reacted quickly and ducked behind a soda machine nearby (they were dorm halls, after all). There were three guys dressed in black that were carrying out some guy… and he appeared to be gagged with a black hood over his head, struggling while the guys briskly moved him down the stairs and (likely) out the front. Kyle stood up and looked at the still-open door. A handsome, bearded, and barefooted college guy stood there, just about to close it. Kyle spoke up:

"Hello?"

"Oh hey – um, can I help you?"

"Yeah, um… is Todd here?"

The bearded guy laughed. "Ha ha – you just saw him leave." He pointed to door that the guys dressed in black just carried the man through.

"Oh, OK. Thanks."

"No problem."

Doug was just about ready to close the door when Kyle found himself blurting out again subconsciously: "Nice feet, by the way." The second he said it, he began walking away in the direction of the secretive men. He could hear the bearded young man behind him say "Wow… another one…"

Exiting the front door of Larguinha Hall, it was obvious that the conversation with the handsome unshod fellow made the trail go a little cold. Kyle looked around, and on the other side of the quad, he could see the three figures (well, four, technically) still moving. Kyle sprinted in their direction – he wasn't about to be seen quite yet, so he could make up some lost ground. Perhaps it was just because the college that Kyle attended was in a small town, but for some reason the sight of three guys in black carrying a third guy in the middle of the night wasn't eliciting any phone calls to police. Maybe people just thought it was another crazy college prank... and maybe it was just another crazy college prank: Kyle wasn't sure. Two block away from campus and there was still no stopping the guys, but, really, it was the middle of the night, so there wasn't much to be done. There was a seedy roadside motel nearby (right off the on-ramp next to the college – the perfect, cheap place for visiting parents to stay), and the men were heading there, moving towards a particular room. Kyle was able to catch them enter what appeared to be room #20, and saw the door close behind them. Yes, definitely room #20. Where was Kyle's "foot twin" being taken? This appeared to be more than just a college prank...

Kyle was struck with fear. Maybe he was dealing with criminals. Or worse. Yet, for whatever reason, he couldn't help but be intrigued. It couldn't be that bad – the bearded barefoot guy seemed pretty ambivalent to the whole thing, so he must've been in on it. Kyle sneaked up to the door of the room, his back facing the parking lot and night air. Kyle pressed his ear up to the door to listen, and could hear bits and pieces of words – usually a lot of cussing from what he assumed was Todd, and phrases like "don't tie me up! C'mon!" Then he heard a deeper, more confident voice ask "So, tell me Todd... are you ticklish?"

Kyle gasped in horrified recognition.

"Did you hear that?" said a voice from inside.

Before Kyle had time to lean away from the door, the door opened, and he fell right onto the floor of the hotel room. He then saw a glorious sight before him: three frat guys dressed in black, the guy from the Facebook worship pictures tied on a bed, and then a muscular, well-built 20-something standing right before him in nothing but surfer shorts, his bare feet screaming of a perfection that Kyle had never seen before in his life. Kyle was humiliated, embarrassed, and dumbfounded… and then he again said something without thinking about it: "nice feet."

The barefooted adonis snickered.

"Oh, this night is getting better and better," he smirked.

Kyle wouldn't set foot outside the room for another dozen hours or so…

————

The three frat boys dressed in black were finally leaving, having just stripped the intruder to his shorts and tying him up stomach-to-stomach with the other boy, positioned specifically as per the request of the half-naked guy in the middle of the hotel room. Said boy locked the door behind the three guys in black as they left. Todd had been gagged to silence his constant complaints (though he was a lot quieter after one of the three guys gave him a jolt to his sides). Kyle did not struggle as his clothes were removed and was tied to the boy he recognized from the Facebook pictures. The unshod athlete type paced the room a bit, then, snickering, removed Todd's gag.

"What the fuck is going on?!" shouted out Todd.

"Oh, you are in no position to be demanding anything, boy." The muscular guy continued to pace around the bed with the two bound boys. "You can call me… the Master. In fact, you will call me the Master… unless you want a good ol' fashioned tickling to straighten you out."

Both boys gulped simultaneously.

"This is all about you, Todd," started the Master. "You fucked with the wrong guy. You may know a kid named Jason, and you may know that he had kind of a thing for you. Well, not you, but definitely your feet… and I can see why." The Master kneeled down and looked at the tied pairs of collegiate boyfeet flinching before him. "You both have very nice sets, I must say – it's just going to make the night all the more fun." The Master laughed. "You see, Todd, all Jason wanted to do was to worship your feet. But no – you had to take advantage of him. You think that after a few rounds of Foot Club, you can tell other people what to do, and how to be… tickled." Todd gulped. "But Jason has got a lot of resources, my friend. And a lot of money. He contacted me via my website, 'cos when there needs to be a guy tickled into reason, I'm the guy to do it. I am the Master, and this is what I do. I was paid a hefty fee by a poor, ticklish college student to seek revenge on egocentric little you, and I intend to get it, my friend. Oh yes. Most people need to eat and breathe in order to sustain life… and I need to tickle. It is one my one release in this world, and until you've seen a horny frat boy beg you for mercy between tears, you don't know what kindness really is. Until you've broken down a high school jock by wiggling your fingers on his ribcage, making him laugh and do whatever you say to stop it… you don't know what real power is. Tickling is the great leveler, as any jock can be ticklish, as can any nerd. Tickling is unbiased: certain boys will be ticklish and certain boys will have that ticklishness used against them. I've tickled cheating spouses, guys too broke to pay bookies, and was even brought in by the CIA once… and I'm only 20 years old, dude. I'm not even in my prime of primes yet! Yet I have tickled so many feet, destroyed so many ribcages, and made so many guys squeal at the discovery that the nape of their neck is in fact the most ticklish place on their whole body… and this is an experience I'm going to share with you, Todd."

The Master turned to Kyle. "And you, whoever you are, well… you're just at the wrong place at the wrong time." The Master snickered again. Kyle only had one thought:

This couldn't be happening.

No, no – there is no way that this could be happening. There the boys were, stripped to their boxers and tied to each other on the hotel bed, stomach-to-stomach. Their hands were wrapped around the other's ribcage, like an awkward-yet-effective hug. Neither could move except for their hands, the guys' bared ankles trapped in an elaborate web of zip-ties. The young 20-somethings looked in each other's eyes and could see that they were experiencing the same feeling: a mixture of excitement and undeniable mortal terror. The hotel wall lamp was all that was lighting their sweat-drenched bodies, and that's exactly how The Master liked it. "OK, boys," the Master started, "one of you is going to be my Tickle Toy for the evening. But I want to see which one wants it more – therefore, you are going to tickle each other into submission. The first one to relent is going to be put in a world of – heh – delights…" The Master snickered. "So it's tickle or be tickled, young squires. Any questions?"

Todd spoke up and said "Yeah…", then turning to his collegiate tickle counterpart (whose fingers were starting to softly circle the area just below Todd's pits). "What's your name?" The other boy laughed a bit: "Kyle."

"Enough of the small talk!" shouted The Master. "Now… BEGIN!"

Four pairs of hands across two young ribcages: it was an explosion of laughter.

Suddenly, the boys were tickling each other, and both were equally ticklish. Neither knew anything about the boy across from them except their name, but it was live or die scenario. Armpit hairs were circled, ribs were prodded, and stomachs were lightly scraped with the fingernails from extended pinky fingers. The boys rolled around on their bed, the Master sitting in a hotel chair, his hand clearly having fun whilst inserted down his surfer shorts. The ticklers were being tickled while tickling, making for a vicious, unending cycle of cruel laughter. Kyle tried his hardest to tickle whilst receiving his worst punishment ever – as long as he kept his hands in motion he'd be fine. Todd, meanwhile, with tears streaming down his cheeks, did the best he could to block out the tickling sensations that were attacking him from all sides, trying to achieve some sort of Tickle Zen while inflicting maximum laughter on his opponent. Only two minutes in, both boys rods began to solidify, and between their boxer shorts, it was like the two boys were jousting during this match, making the tickling all the more potent. The Master was enjoying the spectacle as much as the boys were. The hands weren't stopping, and to some it might look as if the boys had become one giant tickle organism that could only sustain its existence by tickling itself all the time. They were one horny, bound, boxer-clad mass of tickle hormones exploding in every direction at once. Then Kyle found Todd's pecs – and Todd yelped.

"DEAR GOD I CAN'T TAKE IT ANYMORE!!" screamed Todd.

"Yes!" replied Kyle.

"We have a winner!" declared the Master.

Both boys lay on the bed, sweating and taking bucket breaths in unison. Their lips were positioned dangerously close to each other, but neither noticed – they were too exhausted to notice. The Master used some scissors to remove the zip-ties, and soon both boys were free, still lying on the bed, unable to move. The Master picked up Kyle and laid him down on the floor facedown. "Lick my feet every time I walk by" he ordered. Kyle weakly nodded. Todd, still on the bed, was soon tied spread-eagle, the Master walking around the bed multiple times just to make sure that the restraints were as tight as possible, the Master slowing his step (sometimes ridiculously so) when he neared Kyle's mouth… and Kyle's lizard tongue appeased the Master every time (the Master actually liked the tops of his feet to be licked moreso than the bottoms). Soon, Todd was bound and unable to move a single inch. The Master looked down at the floor-hugging Kyle.

"OK, what's your name again?"

"Kyle."

"No, your name is Slave for the rest of the night. Now I'm gonna wash up before we start – I want you to prep Todd's feet for me."

"Um, how do I do that?"

The Master wiggled his perfect toes. "The same way you prepped mine, Slave."

As the Master went into the restroom to get himself ready, Kyle crawled over to the first bare foot he could see tied to the corner of the bed. He looked at it – sweaty, unmoving, and perfect. Kyle picked himself up to a kneel, soon placing his nose right between Todd's big and first toe, his nostrils treated to a symphony of foot delights. Todd, so out of it, actually laughed as he felt the air being drawn up to Kyle's nose on his toes. Then, came the licking. Kyle started out slowly, dabbing Todd's toepads like a painter placing a brush to an easel to grab the first few bits of watercolor. Then, Kyle's tongue began working around the toepads to touch the top of the toenail, polishing it. The tongue continued to circle, soon focusing on the spaces between the toes, like a slimy dragon weaving through a forest of trees. Todd felt the ticklish pleasures, but was so out of it his toes couldn't even flinch in reaction. His feet belonged to Kyle. That tongue… it just didn't stop! It was exploring every inch of Todd's already-sensitive, already-ticklish toes, soon taking a trip down through the valley that was Todd's high arches. Todd could only sit there and take it like a man. Now that Kyle had warmed up, he was ready to lick the second foot with even more force.

"Enough, Slave!"

Kyle cowered next to the Master's commanding voice. The Master walked up to the bed, kneeling between Todd's now spread legs, Master's full weight bowing the bed, his own feet sticking out on the edge.

"Slave," he commanded "I want you to service my feet as I begin my process with this young… toy."

Slave obliged.

As Kyle began engulfing the Master's toes, the Master's fingernails began lightly scraping around Todd's belly button. They danced and drifted, twisting and tangling his happy trail with joyous ease, then floating over to Todd's inner thighs. It was here that Todd's body tried to fold up into itself, but to no avail. Noticing, the Master continued to focus on the inner thighs, stroking in a fashion that was both loving and unbelievably devious at the same time. The nails soon began sneaking right under the rim of the boxers, and Todd's boner could stand it anymore. Through the boxer fabric, the fingernails began lightly tormenting the tent pole, and Todd went from giggling to begging in a second flat. Those devious little fingernails... they just were focusing on every single weak spot that Todd knew. The Master's own hardon was raging through his shorts – after all, he was having his feet licked while tickle torturing a hot young boy – but those fingernails weren't satisfied with Todd's horniness. They soon crept back to the belly button... then to the bottom of Todd's ribcage. Still dancing. Feather-light tickling was the bane of Todd's existence, and it didn't take long for the Master to figure that out. "Oh, you're a fun one, aren't you, Todd?"

Two hours later, Todd's boxers had been cut off by scissors, and Kyle had his hands tied behind his back, ordered to now tickle Todd's feet with his tongue. Even though Todd was spread-eagled on the bed, the Master had somehow slid himself underneath the space between the bed and Kyle's spread-eagled body – Todd's helplessness was increased ten-fold as this tickle urchin existed beneath him, feeding off of his laughter and nothing else. Todd's mind had broken – time and space no longer existed for him: he was just one giant erogenous tickle zone whose sole purpose in life was to be tickled. The hands from underneath played with his neck and underarms and the small of his back. Then, they were tickling the base of Todd's cock.

"Slave!" Master ordered. "Come here and wiggle your fingers under his balls." The horny, pre-cum-soaked Todd couldn't stand it anymore, and as soon as Kyle's fingernails began dancing under his balls, Todd's body accepted defeat, shooting the biggest wad of cum ever to emerge from his lanky frame. Rifle shots, practically. The shooting came in waves, each new one slightly weaker then the last. Yet as he shot, Master's hands began working their way back to his ribs, and right as Todd was leveling from his euphoric climax, the tickles began to start all over again, and they were worse than before, his own body turned into a weapon against him. Todd lasted for one more minute… then passed out.

———————

It was morning. Kyle and Todd were both asleep, themselves tied stomach-to-stomach again, but this time head to toe. In fact, their toes were lightly inserted into each other's mouths… and the backs of their heads were duck-taped into place around the opposing boy's ankles. In fact, both boys, groggily waking up while chewing lightly on the other's toes, noticed that they were tied up again, but why duct-tape? The answer was simple: the Master was gone.

"You awake, Todd?"

Todd groggily managed a "yes", somewhat muffled by Kyle's toes between his lips. Kyle moved a bit, hands duct-taped behind his back. He managed to wriggle free, then helped Todd. Kyle noticed his shorts were gone too… in fact, the hotel room was empty. The clothes both boys started here with were gone. Both boys only had shards of duct tape to conceal themselves with, but that wasn't enough.

There was a knock on the door.

"Housekeeping!" shouted a voice.

Kyle ran to double-lock the door.

"Not now!" he said. "Come back later!"

Close one.

Todd, still weak, rolled onto his stomach, back facing the ceiling. Kyle looked at Todd's back, and it had the phrase "Tickledum" written on it. Todd approached closer… wait, it wasn't written… it was tattooed. Man, the Master was serious… but what did "Tickledum" mean? Suddenly, Kyle's eyes widened. He jolted to the restroom and tried to look at his back in the mirror... and he could make out the backwards word "Tickledee". No. This couldn't be.

Kyle shamefully walked back to the bed and sat on it next to Todd's nude body. Todd mumbled some words out:

"Hey dude, where are our clothes?"

"I think the Master took them, Todd."

"Well… fuck."

"Yeah, I know."

There was a pause. Todd's strength was slowly returning. "Hey Kyle…"

"What?"

"Thanks for last night."

"… um… what?"

"That… that was the most intense experience I ever had in my life. It was… incredible."

"Same here, buddy."

"You got kind eyes, you know that?"

"Heh, yeah."

Another moment. Kyle craned his neck down to Todd's face. They kissed.

Tickledee and Tickledum had never been happier.

STONED INDIFFERENCE

I'm not going to advocate any sort of drug-use whatsoever here, but the use of ganja can certainly make you open to more "exciting" experiences. Your body's sensitivity and reception towards pleasure, for example, is heightened to an unfathomable degree. As such, stoned tickling (hell, even stoned foot-worship) is mind-blowing. This was a story that explored this notion to its logical conclusion, and, well, let's just say I wouldn't be envious if I was one of my own characters in this one...

Lee's flip-flops were about to fall off. This wasn't a good thing.

Elevated about a solid foot off of the ground, Lee was being pressed up against the wall outside his college cafeteria by a bulky, buzz-cut young jock named Andy. Andy's forearm was pressing right up into Lee's chest. Lee, being the geeky English major that he was, could do nothing but play puppet to his overly-aggressive handler.

"Gimme the goddamn card, Nerdlinger!"

"C'mon – these last meals are for me!" said Lee as best as he could through his presently-squished face. His left flip dropped to the floor.

"Do you want to look good for your online girlfriend or not?" bellowed Andy, his two jock friends behind him snickering at the remark.

Reluctantly, and without much choice, Lee handed over his meal card to Andy. Andy released the shy freshman, who immediately dropped to the ground. Gasping for air, Lee could hear Andy make some snidely stupid remark as he entered the cafeteria with his meal card: "Dropped your sandal, Nerdlinger." Almost on cue, Lee could feel his stomach rumble. He was going to be hungry tonight… again.

Angrily walking back to his room, Lee thought about how this whole predicament started. Writing for his college's student paper during his first term, Lee secretly had journalistic dreams, wanting to become a pro music critic – unfortunately, there already was a music columnist at his campus paper named Evan; he had a goofy whiteboy fro but the kid knew what he was talking about, so Lee knew best to stay off. Wanting to break into the journalism clique by any means necessary, Lee talked to the paper's editors (seniors, naturally) willing to take on any story available. Wanting to test him out with a high profile piece his first time out, the seniors had him cover the big homecoming football game. Lee prosed his coverage up to make it as dramatic as possible, but what he failed to realize (as did his copyeditors, who just took him at his word) was that there were two Andy's on the team: Andy Fitzpatrick and Andy Holmes. In his article, Lee wrote that

Holmes had completed the game-winning touchdown… when it was in fact Fitzpatrick (putting Holmes' name in the headline certainly didn't help either). Though the captain of the team fired off a very angry letter to the paper, it was Fitzpatrick himself who would up giving Lee the hardest time: calling him names in passing between classes, writing embarrassing remarks on Lee's Facebook wall, and – as of recent – bullying him into giving him his meal card so that Andy could swipe himself in to the cafeteria. Either Andy lived off-campus or he was just being a dick to Lee… either way, it annoyed him.

Storming into his room, Lee kicked off his flips and jumped right into his bed, burrowing his head into his pillow. His roommate Brandon, who was on his computer, looked over to see his roommate's chest heaving mightily: these were angry breaths. The dark-haired Brandon turned to Lee and asked what any good friend would ask in such a situation:

"What the fuck, man?"

"God, I fucking hate Andy." said Lee, angrily, through his pillow.

"Well, that's not too out of the ordinary. What'd he do this time?"

Lee sat up and faced his roommate: "He took my meal card. AGAIN. This is the fifth time he's done it! I practically had to beg him to get it back from him last time around. He's used up so many that I don't think I'm going to have enough meals to finish out the term. I mean… Christ, it was one typo, man!"

"Well, in his defense, it was a pretty big typo."

"You're not helping, Brandon."

"Sorry dude. I'm just saying."

Lee went face down into his pillow again. Brandon walked over to his roommate and placed his hand on Lee's back.

"Dude, he may be an asshole, but you can't let this stuff get to you. Why don't you go out tonight? Have some fun? Huh? I hear Cindy Dorffman is going to be holding a kickass party at her house tonight. You should go. It's off-campus so you know shit's gonna get wild."

"Are you going?"

"Nah, man. I'm heading back to the city to see my 'rents this weekend. They want to 'restructure my student loan payments' this weekend, whatever that means. I figure I can get some free meals out of it as well, so I figured what the hell."

"When do you leave?"

"Tonight. Why?"

"I dunno," said Lee, facing his handsome roommate again. "Just nice to not be alone sometimes, you know?"

"I know man. Hey – why don't you jack it to one of your tickle videos? That always seems to cheer you up."

"Dude, it's called having a tickle fetish, and sometimes videos just don't match to the real thing, ya know?"

"Well, whatever. I'm just offering suggestions."

There was a pregnant pause. Lee started: "You know, my offer still stands…"

"Ha!" laughed Brandon. "Dude, again, I'm not gay, and even if I were to let you tie me up and tickle me, it'd have to be for more than $100. Though I dunno, we'll see how this whole 'loan restructuring' thing goes, ha ha." Lee was stunned: he actually said 'ha ha'.

Brandon looked at the clock on his cell phone. "Oh shit dude, I gotta go!" He ran to his drawer to get a fresh pair of socks and began putting them on. He turned to Lee: "Ya know, man, if you want that frozen pizza in my mini-fridge, you can have it, dude."

"Really?"

"Pfft, why not. I'll be gone all weekend anyways. 'sides – you're a lot more fun when you're not starving or pissed off."

Lee smiled. "Thanks, roomie."

"Seriously, Lee: have a good time tonight. You can even steal one of my joints if that'll help."

Lee smirked. "You do know you're a good guy, you know that?"

"You're damn right, dude. And don't you forget it." Brandon said that last bit with a smile. Slinging his backpack over his shoulder, he headed for the door. "Catch ya later, Lee."

"Later, man."

The door shut behind Brandon as he dashed out. Lee took a heavy sigh, and laid back into his bed. Before long, he was sleeping.

When Lee woke up, it was well past 9PM. Distraught, he popped Brandon's frozen pizza in the kitchen in his common area, and took a shower while it cooked. When Lee was all dressed again (button T-shirt, jeans, and flips – his favorite look), he helped himself to some pizza, checked his e-mail, some foot and tickle sites, and then his Facebook. His friend Lisa (from AP Lit) did a Facebook invite, asking him to Cindy's crazy party. At least one of his friends would be there if he went. Maybe going would be a good idea, he thought. He finished his third slice of greasy pepperoni pizza, placed the remaining slices in Brandon's mini-fridge, and then made up his mind: he was going to this party. He called Lisa and was soon heading out the door in no time flat.

Meeting the stunning, blonde girl that was Lisa over at her dorm entrance, Lee walked with her as he told her of his latest run-ins with Andy and she told him of how things are getting mixed up with two guys in her poetry class who are best friends but both kinda like her. They had a great understanding. When arriving at the somewhat decrepit house that Cindy lived in, it was obvious that the party was well under way: music was blaring out from the windows, a bunch of guys were casually swigging Bud Lite on the front porch, a girl was already throwing up by the side of the house, etc. Though reluctant, Lee went in, and it wasn't long before Lisa found some other friends and soon branched off, leaving Lee by his lonesome. He made his way upstairs, where it was surprisingly dark. Looking about the open-door rooms, he eventually found a room that was filled with what had to be 20, 25 people. A bunch of people were watching *The Dark Knight* in Blu-ray, and on a big HD TV as well – no wonder the lights were darkened. Most everyone had a beer, but Lee was OK for the time being. He hugged the back wall and just watched with everyone else (some people hadn't seen it yet, so the pencil scene was a great surprise – Lee smiled at their horrified reactions).

Some 20 minutes later, a voice cried out "Hey, I'm hot-boxin' in the bathroom if anyone wants to join." Lee knew what that meant, and yeah, he wanted to smoke up too – this was a night to forget about his worries. He made his way into the cramped little bathroom on the second floor of this house and closed the door behind him. He turned and saw who that voice belonged to: Andy (Fitzpatrick).

"Oh, Nerdlinger."

Lee paused. "Do I have to beg to get my card back this time?"

"Nah," said Andy, who seemed to be in usually good spirits. "Here ya go man." Andy handed Lee his meal card back, as if it were no big deal. This was unusual. Andy looked around the cramped room. "Just you, Nerdlinger?"

"Um, yeah, I guess."

"Man… I thought more people would want to smoke up, I guess. This is kinda disappointing."

All Lee could do was stare at his sometimes-nemesis. He was decked in a red T-shirt, backwards Yankees cap, cargo shorts, and tennis shoes with ankle socks – he was… kind of attractive for the moment. Andy was acting as if all the bullying over the past couple of months was no big deal. In fact, it seemed like Andy hardly knew him at all. Lee wondered if Andy had already had a bowl or two prior.

"Well, hey," said Lee, somewhat nervously, "if people don't want to join in, that just means more grass for us, right?"

Andy laughed a bit. "You're damn right, Nerdlinger. Why spread the wealth, ya know?" Lee actually didn't know, but nodded in agreement anyway. Andy reached to the apple on the small little sink, which, Lee noticed, had been carved out into a makeshift bong. There was a healthy amount of weed on the top, and before long Andy grabbed a lighter and began smoking. He inhaled a deep breath… and then handed it to Lee. Given that the bathroom was, in fact, pretty small, the smoke was accumulating and genuinely "hotboxing", meaning the guys were getting second-hand inhales as well. Lee was going to stop as soon as Andy did, but Andy kept passing the apple back and forth – they must've had ten hits between them! Around the final one, Lee began to feel the effects that the grass was having on him… and this was some potent stuff. Lee began laughing for no reason. Andy turned to him with that goofy stoner grin slapped upon his face.

"What's so funny, man?"

Lee giggled. "I don't know, man!"

"Awesome." The boys laughed and suddenly felt good about… well, everything. Lee started at himself in the bathroom mirror. Then at the door handle for no reason. Then to Andy, who was looking down on the floor for some reason. Lee tried to focus in on what Andy was so intently viewing… and… no. It couldn't be.

Andy was looking at Lee's own toes.

There wasn't a doubt that they looked good in cheap flip-flops and draped in blue jeans as they did now, but Andy looked positively hypnotized by then. Lee wanted to test his theory: he wiggled his toes, and it had a visible effect on Andy: his mouth dropped open, agape in wonder. Lee wiggled again, and Andy took a deep, unconscious breath. Lee wondered if it was true, so tried to – in the stoned haze of his mind – be very careful with what he was going to say.

"Andy… what are you looking at?"

"Oh, um… nothing, man."

"Were you looking at my feet, dude?"

"… no."

"It's OK to say that you were, man."

Andy paused, still staring downward. "OK, I totally was."

"You like 'em?"

"Oh god yes." Andy stared up. "I mean… no I… I don't know."

Lee grinned. "Andy… do you have a foot fetish?"

Andy's face went beat-red. "… maybe."

Lee couldn't stop grinning. "I think you do, Andy."

"Oh god, dude! Please, don't tell anyone! The guys would hate me if they knew I was staring at their feet in the locker room. Promise me you won't tell them, dude!"

Wow, Andy's paranoia was really taking over. Lee, suddenly, had an ingenious idea.

"Sit down." he instructed the jock. Obediently, Andy sat down on the toilet seat. Lee sat down on the edge of the cheap little bathtub installed in this bathroom. Lee raised his sandaled foot and placed it right in Andy's lap.

"OK, Andy – I'll keep your secret... but only if you worship my foot."

Andy, stoned out of his gourd, got an excited look on his face. "Really?" Somewhere in the back of his mind, Lee knew that were they not as baked as they were, this wouldn't even be happening. Right now, however, it was turning into a fantastic, erotic dream.

"Yes, Andy – really."

Andy cupped Lee's foot in his hands, and slowly, carefully, removed Lee's sandal and let it slap against the tile floor. Lee looked up: pot smoke was still circling the horny young men. Cautiously, Andy elevated Lee's foot up to his nose, and inserted his nostrils right at the base of his big toe. Andy inhaled, and Lee could see it was affecting him deeply. While one hand held onto Lee's foot, Andy's other hand immediately clutched his own crotch area, feeling for some sort of erection lost in cargo-short jungle. Lee was blown away: Andy got a hardon simply by smelling his foot. Slowly, Andy's tongue darted out to Lee's toe-pad, and it felt glorious. First the tongue was licking the ends of Lee's toes, almost cautiously, but a few moments later, the jock's big, moist, meaty tongue was darting inbetween Lee's small forest of blonde toehair, slithering inbetween the spaces between his toes. Lee leaned back, and tried his hardest not to think of his own instant boner... but being as high as he was, that hardon was about all he could think of. His toebath felt like the best thing he had ever felt in his life, and giving how Andy's free hand was continually adjusting something underneath his shorts, Lee surmised that Andy was enjoying himself as well. Then it call came to a grinding halt.

knock knock knock "Hey, is someone in there? I need to go!"

Andy's face shot up. He immediately dropped Lee's foot and ran the apple-bong underneath the sink faucet to try and get all the residue out. Lee slid his moist foot into his flip again, and soon both boys exited the bathroom while some other guy rushed in and closed (and locked) the door behind him. Standing in the dim hallway, Lee noticed an erection making itself known in Andy's shorts. Lee looked at Andy and, without any hesitation, said simply: "Back to my place?" Still stupidly grinning, Andy nodded. If Lee wasn't as stoned as he was, he'd be amazed by how easy it was to convince his nemesis to do such wonderful things…

———————

When they got back to Lee's room, only the glow of Lee and Brandon's dual screensavers was illuminating the small dorm that Lee called home. As soon as Andy entered and Lee locked the door behind the both of them, Andy – stupid, stoned, and very horny – turned to the small geek and asked simply "OK – how do we do this?"

Lee, enjoying the slight roleplay from earlier, clumsily said whatever came out of his mouth.

"Well, first off, how can a slave worship the feet of his master if the slave himself is not barefoot?"

"Of course, master!" said Andy, who kneeled down and was able to slide both his sneakers and his ankle socks off in one go. Were Lee sober, he would've noticed a few things already: 1> Andy jumped right in by calling him 'master'. 2> Back in Cindy's house, Lee said 'worship' and Andy knew exactly what it meant. And 3> holy shit,

Andy Fitzpatrick had a goddamn foot fetish and had already given his toes a tonguebath! Andy, now nursing his own rod of steel, wanted to see just how far he could go.

Andy looked eager: "May I worship master's feet now?"

Lee was severely enjoying this roleplay. "No! First, you must answer me… what do you want to do to my feet?"

"Oh man" started Andy's stoned, horned-up monologue, "what wouldn't I want to do to them? I want to lick them and kiss them and suck on your toes and lick them and tie you up and tickle you and have your feet sticking out over the edge of your bed while still in jeans and rub my cock along the tops of your feet just so that your foothair stimulates it just enough and then cum all over you and then lick your num-nums all over again!"

4> Andy just called Lee's toes 'num-nums'.

"OK," started Lee, "you may do so, but FIRST! Tell me… how ticklish are you?"

Andy yelped, completely out of character. "Oh god, very."

"Well then, how much tickling will you be willing to endure to live out your fantasy?"

"Oh man, I dunno…"

Lee jumped on his bed, his legs hanging off the side, facing Andy. He let his flips drop to the floor. He purposely rolled his feet around in the air just to see how hypnotized his stoned little jock friend was. Andy's tone was changing:

"Well, god… they're just so goddamn beautiful. I dunno… I'd do anything just to get to taste 'em again."

"That's all you want to do? To taste them?"

"To taste them and worship them and fuck them and lick them all over again, yes master."

"Then take your shirt off and lay on my bed, slave. You need to be tied up first."

"Yes, master."

5> Andy was letting himself get tied up for tickling just so he could taste Lee's feet. Fucking wow.

6> Andy automatically put his arms over his head, as if he knew what position to be tied and tickled in.

Lee went into his dresser and found the longest dress ties he could find. He soon began securing Andy's arms to the bed's frame, and then moved over to Andy's feet. Lee had to stop for a moment – he was glaring at the tops of Andy's feet, and they were glorious. Huge, size 12 monsters with wonderful-looking toes, and just the perfect amount of hair on the tops. Lee was getting turned on all over again, as if there was an erection inside his erection (which was now threatening to rip a hole in his jeans. After he secured the anxious jockboy, Lee pulled out one other tie and began to blindfold his newfound footslave.

"Oh, c'mon, man! I can't see!"

"That's kind of the point" said Lee, who – now that Andy was blindfolded, began stripping down to his boxers. Lee jumped up on his bed and straddled Andy right at his midsection. Already the jock was struggling. Lee began asking a series of questions to which he already knew the answer to.

"Do you like being tickled, my slave? I bet you love being tickled. Where are your ticklish spots?"

Grinning, Andy yelled "I'm not telling you!"

"Well we'll just have to find out now won't we?" And like an eager miner, Lee's index finger slowly descended into Andy's belly button. When their skin made contact, Andy screamed.

"DON'T!"

"Oh, it's too late, tickle slave!"

Lee's finger began twisting and contorting within that belly button, like a hungry tickle worm searching for subterranean wells of tickle juice. Lee was relishing the moment: with each move of his finger, he could see Andy's body writhe in accordance. Soon, the finger exited and both hands began lightly spider-tickling the jock's stomach, sending Andy into giggle convulsions. As the hands slowly, carefully worked their way up his ribcage like a ladder made of laughter, Lee began saying diminutive, simple things to make his stoned acquaintance feel even more powerless:

"Who's my tickle toy? Who likes being tickled? Hey everyone – laugh if you want to be tickled!" (Andy's jaw looked almost unhinged. His midsection began thrusting in horny desperation as tickle victim.) "Sounds like we have someone who wants to be tickled! Don't worry, Andy: we got bags and bags of tickles here for you, and we're going to use each and every one on you! So much tickling! Tickle tickle tickle tickle! You're such a good tickle toy. I'm just gonna keep on tickling you until you stop laughing… which is going to be a long, long time, Tickle Toy."

Sweat began collecting in Andy's damp armpits. His toes began twisting and contorting, as if trying to physically release all the tickles from his body. Though still pretty gone, Lee was inhaling these small details, saving them for later. Lee's hands found their way onto Andy's hairy thighs, and they squeezed as if tickle juice would come out. Andy yelped and laughed some more. As far as the blindfolded Andy was concerned, Lee's hands turned back into the dreaded Tickle

Spiders, and they were… going up the legs of his shorts! They were now under his shorts – he couldn't take it anymore!

Lee looked on – the tentpole was so pronounced he could hold a circus under there. As caught up as he was in it, Lee suddenly stopped tickling his victim, and collapsed right next to his bound side, his nose dangerously close to Andy's exposed armpit. Even though he wasn't being tickled, these laughter aftershocks kept coming in waves, and Lee was enjoying each and every one. Lee's devious finger reached over and scratched the top of Andy's tent pole, the sensation felt between a layer of both cargo and boxer fabric. Andy's midsection contracted as much as it could, but it couldn't escape. Lee grinned again, his finger now circling the top of Andy's cockhead:

"Tell me, slave… what do you want to have happen now?"

"Oh god… I need to cum!"

"What was that?"

"I need to cum, master! Oh god I need to cum!"

Positioned parallel to him, Lee's barefeet now began rubbing against Andy's bound feet, almost polishing them.

"Oh, you need to cum, do you? I thought you wanted to worship my feet… "

"I want to do both!"

"Well, you can have both, but only under one condition."

"What's that?" said Andy, desperate, pleadingly.

"You gotta suffer through more tickling."

"Noooooooo!"

"No? Well no cumming or toe-sucking for you..."

"No no – it's ok! You can tickle me! Tickle me to your hearts content... but goddammit let me cum!"

Lee noted what he was doing: maybe the foot-foot rub and the cockhead circling was too much... especially at the same time. He whispered to Andy "OK, Tickle Toy. Walk me through what you want me to do." The finger was still circling. Both were still horny and fantastically stoned.

"OK OK OK OK OK... stop circling for a second. OK. Now. Undo my shorts button. OK. Now pull the zipper down... slowly. Oh yeah. That feels so goddamn good. OK. Pull the shorts down. No, further. OK. Now... god... pull my shorts down. Yeah. Oh god. OH GOD my cock feels free."

Lee's hands tweaked Andy's nipples slightly.

"OH god no! OK OK... now... um... rub your big toe along my shaft."

Lee's finger instead lightly circled the massive, meaty cut cockhead of Mr. Fitzpatrick. "Are you sure about that? Looks like you could burst right about now."

"I'm about to!!"

Lee's finger stopped. He swung his feet over so they were now facing the still-blind Andy. He placed both feet right near the jock's face.

"Sniff."

Andy did, and his hips rose with his inhale. Andy's cock was even harder now. Lee readjusted himself and took his big toe and placed it right at the base of Andy's cock... and began dragging it up... slowly... centimeters at a time... and, just like that, Andy came. Hard. Gushing.

Shot after shot. Lee got off his bed, his own hardon straining through his boxers. He stood on the other side of his room and evaluated what was going on: this horny young jock boy who had tormented him so frequently as of late just came after hours of tickle torture and a single toe against his cock. This was, unreal. In fact, the joyous stoner haze he had on before was starting to fade.

Suddenly, Lee was a bit scared, as if he was starting to get sober, then surely the post-orgasm Andy was starting to feel that same way as well... and Christ, what would he do if he suddenly realized that he was tied to a bed in a room he didn't know, covered in cum and Nerdlinger staring at him with a hardon in his shorts? Lee thought about running or untying or... no.

Lee caught a glimpse of Andy's soles, perfect and glorious, in the light of his screensaver. They looked... godlike. Lee's hardon was still raging, and he had to satisfy it. He hadn't even pleasured himself to Andy's feet yet! Then, suddenly, he remembered what Brandon had said. Reaching down in Brandon's cigar box, he pulled out a perfectly rolled joint, and just grinned.

He walked over to his still-bound, still-blind victim, placed the joint to his lips, held up the lighter, and said "inhale." Andy did, and he took a massive, massive hit. Lee smoked even more. He was buzzing again, and no doubt Andy was as well. Tired, blindfolded, and completely helpless, Andy's face turned to where (he thought) Lee was, and said "Can I worship your feet now?"

Lee grinned, setting the spliff down in Brandon's ashtray on his desk. He turned to Andy, staring at those size 12 monsters, and simply said "Ya know, I hear you get more ticklish after cumming."

———————

The "Noooo" that followed would echo in Lee's life forever – he heard nothing louder, nothing more desperate, and nothing as satisfying. Lee was loving being a 'Ler...

MY TICKLISH REVENGE

Without question, this is the most personal, painful story I have ever written. The events in the first couple of paragraphs, in fact, are verbatim what had happened to me with a real-life friend. It's a situation that I had been bitter about for some time, despite my best efforts to suppress it. Ultimately, these feelings manifested themselves into this story, which was a very, very cathartic writing experience, and my first move into "darker" subject matter. It was a pretty "raw-nerve" approach to things, but I sure as hell felt better after completing it. Now if only I could make it happen in real life…

Doug was smoking a cigarette outside. No, scratch that: Doug was angrily smoking a cigarette outside.

He was sitting right in front of his parking space in front of his apartment. It was around 1AM, the moon was out and lighting the night sky, while the 26-year old sat there in exile. A great drunken night of sex with his girlfriend had turned into a great big drunken post-sex argument with his girlfriend. They fought, she broke his glasses, and then proceeded to kick him out of the very apartment they rented together. The night sky was chill, and Doug was shivering: he only had on his ratty old black The Who T-shirt, his light-blue jeans with big knee holes, and his long cotton socks and black shoes. This is how I've come to see Doug more than once. This wasn't the first time I had been called over to be mediator to this troubled couple's arguments. This isn't the first time I've seen the young guy locked out of his apartment by his psychotic partner. This isn't the first time he's reached out for help. This will be the first time I don't help him, however.

Doug and I were insanely good friends. Unbelievably so. Thought-predictingly, sentence-finishingly good. That is until that one night. That one, drunken night. The night when I got candid with him, told him about my foot fetish. He was very nice about, not fully understanding but certainly responding well to the news, asking a few questions but generally humoring me about the only real secret I was hiding from him. Of course, he didn't know I had always fantasized about his feet: his size 9, soft-as-hell, slightly furry on top feet that just drove me up the fucking wall. Doug always had a well-kept beard that he maintained, and it was usually that and his lightly hairy hands that always reminded me of those perfect-looking podicial treasures. I say "reminded" because he was always "self-conscious" about his feet. He rarely, if ever, went barefoot. He owned sandals but pretty much never donned them. He was a shoe guy, by and large. As such, his soles were kept in mint condition: soft, clean, and so fucking unbelievably ticklish.

Yet I didn't tell him all this. His girlfriend, however, was eavesdropping: listening in. She misunderstood so much, burst into the room, called me "faggot" and the top of her lungs, and demanded I leave her house. This news surprised the both of us, and an argument soon ensued. Bitch then broke my cell phone just because. Everyone walked away bitterly. When I finally saw Doug a week later, he was cold, distant. For some truly inexplicable reason, he had taken her side on everything. He felt "betrayed" for some reason, and I couldn't figure out why. That distance turned into bitterness, and I still didn't understand why

I had just lost my best friend. He continued on as nothing happened. To say I was resentful would be an understatement.

Which leads us to why tonight was so weird. He called me up to inform me he got locked out (again) and needed to find a place to crash. I recommended my place (which he stayed at before), but he felt "uncomfortable" around me. "So why did you call?" I asked. "'cos I have no one else to talk to" he replied. I didn't understand it. Positively none of this made sense. Yet even with everything, I still considered him a friend. I drove out to help him. I let him into my car. He put out his cigarette and got in, still shivering somewhat. We started driving off – with no particular destination in mind – and I was trying to figure out what happened. He and his girlfriend were fighting again (nothing new), but this time it was about me for some reason. His explanation soon turned into a tirade: he kept on asking why I had to fuck everything up for him, to which I sat there dumbfounded and confused. Apparently he hadn't gotten over the alleged "incident", despite the fact that nothing had happened. I did my best to contain my anger, but he kept badgering me without any legitimate basis.

I had enough, pulled over the side of the road, and got out. He got out too, and continued yelling at me, asking why I had to even get involved in his life. I reminded him that we used to be good friends and it was just as much his deal as it was mine but apparently that wasn't a good-enough explanation from him. He then started mocking me, and I began to really question why I was called in the first place. The hate that was spewing out of his mouth – I couldn't stand it. I selfishly thought of all the good times we shared, all the bars we used to drink at, all the movies we had rented and drunkenly mocked. He had developed a selective memory about all of that, apparently. I was not only a stranger to him: I was point of hatred. At that point, I had had enough. While he stood next to the passenger-side door extolling his hate-speech, I popped open the trunk, and grabbed a bottle of chloroform. I took a breath in – taking in full understanding of everything that was about to happen – and then released. I opened up the bottle of chloroform, pulled a dusty rag from the trunk space, dipped just the right amount in it, sealed up the bottle, and closed the trunk, rag in hand. I walked right over to Doug – still talking for some reason – and pressed the rag right up to his mouth in mid-sentence. He struggled for a moment, but things happened too quickly. Within five seconds, he was out. He collapsed on the ground by the side of the road. Fortunately at this hour, there weren't many cars around, and I suspect the ones that were just thought he was drunk. I hoisted him back into the car, and strapped him in. I couldn't believe it: I was getting a tear in my eye. God, how I hated that I was doing this, but I had to be honest: one can only take so much abuse for so long before one snaps. I had been Mr. Nice Guy long enough. Now, it was time for him to feel alone and isolated – at my hands, of course…

———————

When Doug woke up, the first thing he noticed was the taste: slightly smelly, very colorful, and very strange. Textured. Cotton-y. Oh yes: I only hope that he would realize that it was my work socks from that very day that were jammed into his mouth. He tried moving his tongue, but all he did was just lick more toe sweat. The sock had then been taped over his mouth, so he couldn't do jack about it. The second thing he noticed was that he couldn't move. His hands were tied very tightly behind his back. Very tightly. He wasn't feeling rope-burn, but he sure as hell couldn't move his hands. Then, of course, were his legs. Dude was still fully clothed – he even still had his shoes on! – but his jeans were providing nice cover: his ankles were tightly duct-taped, and even the area just above his knees was restrained as well. He couldn't spread his legs apart even if he wanted to and his life depended on it. Nope: instead, he was belly down on my big futon in my own apartment, helpless as a baby seal. He could move his legs up and down if he wanted. He could even do The Worm. That was about it. He tried making muffled noises, but all he was greeted with was silence. He looked around. It was obviously my apartment, but everything was dark. He tried screaming through his gag, he tried struggling against his bonds, but it was totally useless: he was helpless. He was mine.

After about 10 minutes of fear-induced hysteria, I turned on a small lamp near the foot of the futon (and where his feet were). He tried looking, but the belly-down position didn't give his neck much arc. He tried to see what he could, but that's when I spoke up. "Hey there Doug. It's me." He struggled some more. "Yeah, I know. I'm sorry buddy, but you're home now. And, well, you're gonna be here for awhile." Struggling again. I sat on the futon, my lap about a foot away from his writhing legs. Those somewhat-worn shoes not even knowing where they'd end up in a bit.

Doug was obviously a bit angry, but I let him have his moment. "Listen up, dumbass," I said in a somewhat-menacing tone, "Do you want to know what's going to happen to you?" His neck arced as much as it could and he glared at me. I smiled. "You see Doug, I've been patient with you. I've been patient as hell, really. When you and your girlfriend decided to shaft me for virtually no reason whatsoever, I took it in stride. I know some friendships cannot last forever, and I obviously hit a button with you. I'd apologize, but I don't really know what to apologize for. For being myself? For treating you like the good guy that I know you are? It's hard to say, really. Yet when I get this call out of the blue after dealing with you ignoring me for months, when I pick you up – yourself obviously still liquored up as hell – and have to deal with nonsense, accusations, and lies flying out of your mouth, what am I supposed to do, Doug? Smile? Thank you for the favor? Need I remind you of my broken phone? Of being called "faggot"? Of all the isolation and loneliness you forced upon me? All I wanted was an explanation and I never got one, despite reaching out to you. And now you want me to house you again but you can't trust me enough to stay with me? Well I've had it, good friend. I've gone way beyond the limit of casual generosity for you. Right now, I get to be jealous. I get to be selfish. I get to… teach you a lesson." Struggling, take 6. "And oh yes, Doug, it's going to involve your… feet."

The neck arced again: now his eyes were wide – with terror.

I grabbed his jeans by the belt loops, and used that to toss him around, the boy now belly-up. I stood up and got more duct-tape. I grabbed him by the ankles and pulled his body down so that his legs were just barely over the wooden edge of the futon. I looped the tape through the gap between his ankle-tape and knee-tape, essentially isolating his feet to just barely be sticking out over the edge of the futon. I taped and taped – Doug was not going anywhere tonight. He still tried struggling on occasion, but already his energy was starting to waver. I was becoming alarmingly pleased with how things were going. I pulled over a chair, and sat right in front of his feet. He tried wavering them around from the ankles, but his movement was extremely limited. I knew just what it'd take to put him over the edge…

I gripped his left shoe with my hand. He got panicked. My grip tightened. I could feel the foot inside trying to break my hold – like a moth trapped inside a mason jar – but it was no use. I was owning this boy tonight. I grabbed his right one now, and he fidgeted and panicked like any good victim should. All I did was hold those shoes in place until the fluttering feet inside calmed down. Once they did, I simply ran my hands up and down the tops of his shoes, just to make his own feet feel like they're objects: like they're not even his anymore. He struggled so more, but, again, to no avail. Also, not as much struggling this time: this was all a good thing. It was almost as if he was resigning to his fate.

Both my hands made their way to his laces, and began slowly pulling those knots undone. I talked as I did so. "So, as you know Doug, I have a male foot fetish. It's huge. It's gigantic. If this were real life, I would be paying you hundreds of dollars just to do what I'm doing right now for free. Yeah, a foot fetish is homoerotic – I'm not going to deny that – but 'faggot'? No, not as much so. I know you're 'self-conscious' about your feet being unshod, but Christ man – you can't hide those things from me forever. They're just too fucking amazing. I think after all the shit I've been through, I deserve a little treat, don't you?" He tried screaming through his gag. It was beautifully muffled. The undone laces now dangled downward. I loosed up the tongues on both of them. "Look at me, Doug." He didn't. "LOOK AT ME!" I yelled in a threatening baritone. He stopped… and craned his head upwards. Our eyes met.

"Think about everything I've been through. Think of all the isolation that you put me through. Think of everything I lost because of you. Think about how you called me tonight, and think about everything that you said." A moment passed. I then very quietly said to him "Doug, if our roles were reversed, wouldn't you do the same?"

The look that he gave me wasn't one of acknowledgement or resentment. He probably wouldn't do the same if our roles were reversed, but he knew that he wasn't a completely blameless creature at this moment. He just gave me the slightest of nods. He knew. He understood. He didn't condone, but he understood. In truth, that took me by surprise. He didn't have to. He should've been angry still. I stepped away for a moment, and then came back with an sleeping eye-mask. I placed it over his eyes. "You don't need to see what happens next, buddy."

He muffled some things but I sure as hell couldn't understand (nor did I care to hear). I unzipped and pulled off my own jeans at this point: I had been sporting a hardon ever since he woke up. I didn't take off my boxers just yet – I wanted to play with my toy, first. I went to his left shoe, wrapped my hands around it, and pulled it off very, very slowly. This was deliberate: I wanted to make each moment unbearable for him. Molasses was faster than this. I just wanted him to feel his meager protection slipping away from him. Past the ankle, the sole, the toes – it was off. The socked foot in front of me wiggled a bit – it was breathing. I did the same to the other foot, and then boom: I had two socked Dougfeet right in front of me. Oh boy. This was fun. I examined the soles of his socks: there foot impressions. Right around the toes and the arch and heel: he had been wearing these socks all day today (even during sex earlier? who knew!). I went and placed my nose just an inch away from his soles, and could just feel the sweaty warmth radiating from them. I then took a big sniff inward. A symphony of erotic flavors had entered my brain. I got drunk off those feet in mere seconds. I was excited. I was in ecstasy. Yet this wasn't enough. I then pressed my nose right into his toes and inhaled. I had become a smell hound, and he was the prey. By physically pressing myself into his feet, he couldn't help but feel a bit violated, but that was the point: these weren't his feet anymore – they were mine.

I sniffed and sniffed and even lightly jerked myself while doing so. This was heaven. He muffled and struggled, but to no effect: my hunt for his footstink was just too great. Perhaps it even smelled better knowing how desperate he felt: maybe there was some fear sweat creeping in as well. Then I sat back on the chair again. I prepped my index finger. It inched closer to the ball of his left foot. Then, I scratched it.

His whole body lurched. The wonderful thing about keeping your feet in shoes all the time: they become soft – and sensitive. Even with that thin layer of cotton between his skin and my fingernail, he could still feel the tickle running through him like a bolt of electricity. It returned again. He jumped again. Then I prepped all 10 nails to start lightly scratching at the balls of his feet. Within seconds, his whole body was writhing again. Holy fuck: he was even more ticklish than I was. Scratchy scratchy scratchy went the nails. The feet tried to cross in front of each other to prevent the attack, but it was no use: the Tickle Spiders were winning. Slowly they moved up his soles, right to the base of his toes, still lightly scratching back and forth, back and forth. I could make out deep-throated laughter even through the gag. Oh, I was getting to him. Yet the Spiders were in no hurry: my hands took their time dishing out Doug's tickle punishment. Next thing he knew, they were playing with his toes. They weren't tickling as much as they were just playing: dancing up and around, poking inbetween (even with the socks in the way), and then quickly scampering down to his ankle again. Then back up. Then down. Then more tickly scratches. This continued for about 20 minutes. It went by like 30 seconds for me... I can't imagine how long it felt for him.

"Awww," I said as I turned to him taking a pause. He was breathing heavily through his nose. "I think you put up with a lot already, haven't you Doug?" He nodded in panicked agreement. "I think we should reward you, shouldn't you?" His head shook vigorously. "Well, I know you pretty well," I started, "and if I'm not mistaken, you just love... being..." I stretched each pause out longer. He was sweating with anticipation. "Bare..." His eyes widened. "... foot."

He screamed so hard. I could almost hear it through the gag this time! I knew each second was slowing down into a torturous minute with him, and I fucking loved it. I was going to break Doug's spirit, and I hadn't even gotten started yet. I sat down again – he was still moaning – and I pinched the little bit of sock between his index and big toe. I did this for both socks. "Ready for liftoff?" He screamed "Noooooooooo!", and I laughed. With firm grip, those socks were coming off slowly. The sock rims sliding down his leg... then around his ankle and heel... and up the sole. His feet were pointed upwards, so by the time the sock rims were just above the toe base (and totally not touching any Dougfoot at all), I just let them dangle there, like a cotton bell, around his toes. They weren't on his feet, technically, but the socks still covered up his toes just dangling there. I wanted him to feel his last bit of protection just barely, barely within reach. I just let the socks dangle for well over a minute, tempting and teasing him. And then, I threw them aside. Doug was now barefoot. Barefoot. Barefoot.

Oh god what a sight.

The toes stretched like how your arms do when you first get out of bed in the morning. They were only covered by air now. Those hairs on the tops of his feet – god, so sexy. And those soles: so perfectly shaped. So beautiful to look at. And they were here, in front of me. They were here, ready to be... tickled.

Without warning, my hands had become Tickle Spiders again, and they lightly whipped along the soles of his feet. Then the sides of his feet. Then the tops of his feet (my favorite part). Then, I cupped both ankles in my hands, freed up my index finger for each, and just let that finger scratch and scratch and scratch. It was like a Scratch-and-Sniff lotto ticket in a way: I scratched 'em, then sniffed his toes. He must've felt so used right about now, but that was kind of the point. My hardon was now raging like a maniac at this point. The index-finger kept scratching and I could hear him chortling and giggling through his gag. I looked over, and saw the biggest smile stretch across his face, and I smiled myself. He had no control over his emotions anymore: I did, and right now I felt like Doug should be laughing. I stuck my nose right next to that big toe on his right foot and inhaled. Then his left. Then his right again. Then his left again. Man, I could keep this up for hours.

"Feel used yet?" I asked. He gave me a "Mm-hmm" that was almost through tears. God this was fun.

I went over to a nearby drawer and pulled out some bird feathers. Nothing much, but just something fun to tease him with. I began feathering the sides of his ankles, and kept that up for five solid minutes. I know what that feels like: it almost tickles but not really but still kinda does. It's almost like tickle foreplay, your senses getting mad before finally crying out "JUST TICKLE ME ALREADY!" The feathers then messed with his toe hairs, then inbetween his fun boytoes, then up and down his soles. He kept laughing and his body (low on energy) still had a spastic twitch here and there. Doug was being worn down into tickle putty. The feathers did their dance, the victim just laid back and laughed.

I stopped, finally, to give him a breather. Every single nerve ending on his feet must've felt on fire. Even though I wasn't tickling him, he was still laughing. Almost like waves upon waves of aftershocks still hitting him. I went to the kitchen and grabbed two water bottles: one for me and one for him. I kneeled down next to the side of the futon and pulled off the tape. Then I slowly pulled my socks out of his mouth. His voice was hoarse. "You… you bastard."

"Have some water" I insisted. Though he still couldn't see, his open mouth eventually found the plastic salvation. He took the water without hesitation, practically draining the entire thing like a hamster in a cage. "Good boy" I told him. I drank some myself. "Please…" he beckoned, all scratchy-sounding. "I give up. Please let me go." It sounded so delightfully pathetic. "Oh but Doug…" I started, "we haven't even got around to lubing your feet yet."

"Noooooo!" said the scratchy, almost non-existent voice.

I went back to my chair near his beautiful Dougfeet. "But wait Doug – I'm all out of lube. Well, you know what I'm going to have to do then, right?" I didn't hear any response. I smirked. I kneeled down next to him so his feet were at face-level. I licked my chops, and planted my moist tongue right at the ball of his left foot, left it there, and slowly drug it upwards. "Noooooooo!" he cried, but it was too late: the worship had begun.

My slow tongue was giving his helpless soles their much-needed saliva. My tongue flickered a bit when it got to his toes. Then it started at the bottom again – on his other foot. I went back and forth licking his Dougsoles, my tongue as Huck Finn's paintbrush and his feet as that endless picket fence in need of a fresh coat. I then went and licked the sides of his feet, his insteps, and then slithered my greedy tongue in-between his toes, savoring every flavor. God this was heaven. His hips thrusted a bit involuntarily, but mostly, Doug was laughing. He's no doubt been tickled before, but not like this. Never like this. He was in pure tickle hell. Plus, the new moisture on his feet was making his skin sensitive to the air around him, the bit of wind in the room occasionally rolling past his sensitive dogs and giving them an extra, bonus tickle. I like bonus tickles.

When I got to his toes, though, god I had a ball. I sucked those things like lollipops, spending extra time flickering his toehairs. Sometimes I'd even scratch his feet while doing so. He was laughing and hating me and probably secretly loving all of this at once. His mind didn't know anymore: it was all confused and irrational. I was controlling it now. I kept sucking and sucking and sucking his toes for well over 20 minutes. Then stopped. I laid down a bit. I looked up at his bound feet. Even through the window, there was a sliver of moonlight bouncing off of his saliva-coated toes now, and it was one of the hottest fucking images I've ever seen. Only now was it time to have fun.

I grabbed some scissors and cut his legs free from the futon armrest. His legs were still bound, but he was no longer in one place. I picked up his body and laid him on the ground face down. I then walked about 15 feet away to the entrance of my apartment. I opened the front door wide open. I put my jeans back on (hardon be damned), kneeled in front of him, and pulled off his eyemask. I pointed to the front door. "Alright Doug, I gotta use the restroom, but let's be fair. If you can make your entire body out that door by the time I get back, I'll let you go. How does that sound?" He didn't respond, but I didn't wait up. "Go!" I said. I really did have to use the restroom, so I did.

When I stepped back out, I knew exactly what had happened: Doug, only able to really move his legs, had "wormed" his way 4 feet closer to the door. His head was still about 10 feet away. It was so demeaning to crawl on his belly towards freedom, but I liked it that way. I snuck up behind him and without warning began licking his soles while they were moving. "Noooo!" he cried, and tried to escape as quickly as he could. I kept following and licking. Of course, this was all part of my plan: I wanted him to use up every last remaining reserve of mental and physical energy towards this task that I knew was impossible for him to do. And even if he did make it out, what was he going to do? Go down whole flights of stairs by himself? Stand up and use a phone with his nose? I had merely created the illusion of freedom for him. In his delirious state of mind, the illusion was real enough for him.

As I (quite literally) nipped at his heels, his chin had finally made it out the door. At this point, I then put his legs in an armlock, and then just proceeded to tickle his feet with vigor. Oh, how they squirmed still. Like little creatures. Little bits of life gasping for freedom. And he tried moving, but I was holding him immobile. "Oops, times up!" I cried. Still holding his legs, I simply stood up and dragged his bound body alllllllll the way back to the base of the futon. "Noooooo!" he cried (again – it was becoming his catch-phrase for the night!). I casually walked over to the door and locked it, trying to make the clicking door lock sound as loud as possible.

Now that he was completely on my carpeted floor, I swung him around so that his face was next to the lamp I turned on earlier. I put the eyemask on again, but he was too tired to say… anything. I pulled my chair over and pulled out my cell phone. "OK Doug, do you really want to get out of here?" "Yes," he whimpered, in near tears. "Do you now know how shitty you made me feel?" "Yes" he said. "Why did you do that to me?" His fevered mind couldn't think of anything, which is what I was counting on. "I don't know" he said in desperation. Just the answer I was looking for. "You don't know? Then why did you even do it if you don't know?" A pause. All he could think of: "I don't know." "Well, it's almost all over soon. I just want you to return me the favor that I did for you tonight… and lick my feet."

His face grimaced for a moment, but he knew he had no choice. "OK" he sighed. Even though he was blind and on the floor like a worm, I inched my socked feet ever-closer to his face. "Now take my socks off." Once his face felt the shape of my feet, his mouth bit down on a bit of sock tip, and I pulled my left foot out. Then he did the other one. "Do you like taking the socks off my feet, Doug?" "Yes" he blindly bemoaned, knowing no other answer would've worked. "Now suck on my toes" I ordered. His mouth felt around, and then he engulfed my big left toe. His mouth sucked on it smoothly, simply, steadily. He went around to other toes and licked and sucked them with equal precision. Even for faking this gesture just for me, I would've mistook him for a guy with his own foot fetish any other night of the week. He simply sucked and sucked my digits. I was fucking loving it. I kept badgering him with questions. "Do you like my toes?" "Yes." "Do you love sucking on them?" "Yes, sir." "Say it to me!" "I… I love…

sucking on your toes… sir." "Will you do it anytime I ask?" "Yes, sir."

CLICK. His mouth stopped. "What was that?" he asked. "Hold on a second" I said. A few digits were pressed in my phone, and boom – it was sending to my e-mail inbox. I rewound the minutes-long video I had just been filming, and then held up the playback to his ear: "Do you like taking the socks off my feet, Doug?" "Yes." I stopped it. I could see he was crying a bit. I broke him.

As tears streamed down his face, I grabbed the scissors and unbound him everywhere. His weak, depleted body just lay there. I sat down and nursed his head, stroking it gently. "It'll be alright, Doug. It'll be alright." Within moments he had passed out.

I don't know when he woke up, but I know where he woke up: a cheap motel not too far from his house. I don't know what transpired, but I checked out a cheap room after he passed out, and basically flopped his barefooted body onto the bed. When he awoke, he would've found the shoes he was wearing last night (but no socks – I kept those), and a cheap pair of purple plastic flip-flops with a note, indicating that if he truly was sorry and wanted to give a chance at restarting everything again between us – with full understanding that if it doesn't work, it doesn't work – he should wear those cheap flip-flops into work the next day.

Of course, he and I worked in the same office: that's where we became friends. They had a very strict dress code. Admittedly, he didn't have to change into "shoes" until he clocked in, which is what I was banking on. I was sitting in a manger's office the next day, barely finishing out my opening shift when I glanced out and saw Doug standing in the doorway, himself on a closing shift. His shoes were in his hands. The cheap flip-flops were on his gorgeous feet. We exchanged glances. He nodded. I smiled. He walked off to change.

I had a good feeling about this…

THE MASTER: THE BEGINNING

When I began writing all these delightful little fictions, I had no intention of tying them altogether or making some sort of insular universe in which my characters would inhabit. Yet the response to the character of "The Master" (the story of which was a double-sequel to both "Foot Club" and "Affluent") was overwhelming, and, eventually, I decided to write a prequel of sorts. This is how The Master got his start, but oh boy does he have tales left to tell...

Michael's face was covered in blood.

His vision dazed and somewhat blurry, Michael was staring at the fluorescent lights overhead. A cute blond cheerleader was bending down to examine his eyes. "I think he's OK!" she shouted. A referee soon came over, followed by Michael's coach. After counting how many fingers his coach was holding up (four), various team members helped Michael up. Michael, nose still bleeding, looked around: the gigantic crowd was all staring at him, making sure he was alright – no one had even picked up the deflected basketball yet. Michael was lead to the bench, over a thousand pair of eyes still watching his every move. Michael glanced up at Gene – his fellow reckless teammate who "accidentally" blocked him and elbowed him square in the nose. Gene was Team Captain, a position that Michael – with his incredible 6'5" frame – desperately wanted as well. Gene beat him out for it just last week, but Gene was a bit of a sore winner. Gene's cold eyes were the only unsympathetic pair in the entire gymnasium. Michael looked around for a bit – everyone breathlessly awaiting for a reaction from him – and simply raised a "thumbs up" in the air as high as he possibly could; the whole gymnasium cheered. The game went on, but Michael, quite obviously, wasn't going to play the rest of it.

That event didn't turn Michael into The Master… but it didn't exactly hinder that process either.

See, here's the thing about Michael: guys who are confident command respect – and tall guys who are confident command even more. When Michael went into High School, he was a popular guy. His passion in life was for basketball, but he had developed to love other classes as well: he was really good at debate, and really good at woodshop. He liked constructing things, and he liked being right. Perhaps this is why he didn't exactly reach out for help when he started failing exams in Physics (his least favorite class). He did what he could, but often struggled by with a C average when it came to Physics or Calculus or just about any other class that had excessive amounts of numbers or "formulas".

As one of the tallest guys in school, he got noticed quite a bit – called out in class (when he didn't even raise his hand), mocked by the other jocks who were secretly jealous of him, and definitely, definitely fending off ladies everywhere he went. Every weekend it was a different girl. His parents pretty much let him have the basement of their house, and with the joys of a side-door entrance, it was girl after girl after girl after girl. The truth of the matter was, though, when Michael was done having sex, lying next to whoever the lucky lady was this week, sweat coating his body as his chest rose and fell at a rapid pace, something was... missing. He wasn't sure what, though. Girls wanted to be with Michael (and wanted to please him), but the strip teases, roleplay, and (yes, once) animal costumes just didn't do it for him. Michael had a pretty dominant personality, and he wished that to be expressed in his sexual conquests. The ideas of humiliation and total control – those appealed to him, but he just wasn't sure how to best express those feelings...

———

Lauren may very well have been Michael's sister. Of all the girls in the same sophomore class as Michael, neither could ever get up the courage to sleep with each other. Lauren was one of Michael's closest friends: the one who kept him in line if he went to far, said the wrong thing to the wrong girl, the one who kept him up to date on all the latest gossip in the school (especially if it was about him). Michael, meanwhile, was Lauren's closest male confidant. He helped her with homework (as long as it wasn't math or science related – history he could easily do), he went out to see boring chick flicks with her when no one else would, and he would listen to her ramble even when (horror of horrors) she wasn't talking about something that specifically related to him. Did they ever kiss? No – they had something more important than that, and they both knew it. Little did they know, it was Lauren who would turn sweet young Michael into The Master...

Michael was in his third period shop class – his absolute favorite time of day. It was his period right before lunch, and he loved it because if he really got into a project he was working on, he could just work through lunch until his next period. Every once in awhile, yes, he did skip lunch altogether, but that didn't matter: Michael enjoyed doing a good job, and, man, he was fucking good. His shop teacher (Mr. Newman) loved Michael – he even made him his T.A. halfway through the term. As such, Michael got certain exceptions, like that day when Michael was finishing his work on a dinner chair (which looked professionally-made) and a tear-stricken Lauren – free of a hall pass – walked in and asked Mr. Newman if she could talk to Michael in private. Though this is a generally frowned-upon practice – especially without a hall pass! – Newman let it slide, and Michael was soon called into the hall. When Lauren saw him, she ran up and hugged him, her body heaving and sobbing. Michael – with plastic work goggles still affixed to his forehead – was a bit taken back. He immediately asked:

"Hey, Laur – what's wrong?"

"Michael! I can't believe him!"

Michael's eyebrow arched. "Believe who?"

"Gene!" More sobs ensued.

"What? What's wrong with Gene? You finally realize he was a douchebag?"

Lauren hit his chest, in no need for humor. "Michael, not now! This is serious!"

Michael sat her down against the empty hallway, and sat down right next to her.

"OK, Laur – take a deep breath. OK? Now, tell me what happened."

Lauren calmed down a bit, then plainly spoke: "OK, Steve was flirting with me. You know Steve, the guy on the Varsity basketball team? He was kind of hitting on me in class a bit, but I… I dunno, I just don't like him, you know? He… he asked me if I wanted to go with him to the Halloween Dance, and I said no, and he said why not, and I said because I just didn't like him that much, and he… he didn't like that. This was yesterday. Today Gene walked up to me and he yelled and yelled at me, asking why I was disrespecting his 'bro' and all this kind of stuff. I dunno, he just… he just called me names and was just really, really mean."

As Lauren described a bit more, Michael just got confirmation to what he already knew: Gene was a bully. A prick. A total dumbass. Michael could take an elbow to the face – that wasn't that bad, really. Yet antagonizing his friend? The girl who may very well be his sister? No. That wasn't cool at all. Then, the window opened up, as Lauren made a very simple request:

"Michael?"

"Yes Lauren?"

"I need you to do me a favor?"

"What's that?"

Then, with a genuine menace in her eyes, she said it quite simply: "I need you to make him pay."

Michael's face lit up. Michael, in all honesty, wasn't a mean guy (he was pretty nice, actually), but bullying others around – and for stupid, stupid reasons no less – that just wasn't cool. As petty an issue as this was (and it was petty), Michael was going to help out Lauren. He was going to teach Gene a lesson, and most importantly, it would be a lesson he would never forget.

––––––––––

With the chair finished and a bit more spare time on his hands, Michael began thinking of the most perfect way to get back at a cocky jerk like Gene. His head swam with ideas: get an embarrassing video of him? Prank-trap his locker somehow? Find something to blackmail him with? Really, none of this panned out very well in Michael's mind. Yet three periods after Lauren tearfully pulled him aside, Michael was in his last class of the day: Medieval History. And what was today about? Prisoners... and how they were tortured.

Michael was unique because when he got obsessed with something, he learned every single possible thing he could about it. Though he always flirted with the idea of bringing someone like Gene down a few pegs, Lauren's plea was just what he needed to let his imagination loose. The torture techniques described in his class were pretty graphic ("the rack" didn't sit well with him at all), and as the teacher droned on, Michael soon began kicking around different ways of torture. He couldn't physically harm Gene, as that could lead to lawsuits, himself getting kicked out of school, etc. He'd like to humiliate Gene somehow, but Michael just couldn't think of how. The idea of Gene tied up and at his mercy intrigued Michael, but he was stuck on what to do with a bound Gene after that. Pour candle wax on him? Take photos of him? Apply clothespins to his nipples? As all of these thoughts swirled in Michael's mind, he realized that all of these thoughts had a bit of a sexual undertone... but that didn't scare Michael at all. In fact, it intrigued him. Unfortunately none of these would work either, as any scars or bruises could come back to haunt Michael...

The bell rang. The teacher pointed to the homework assignment on the board, and then said "don't forget to put your garbage in the proper trash receptacle before you leave..."

Receptacle.

Re-sept-tick-ul.

Sept-tick-ul.

Tick-ul.

Tickle.

Michael's face lit up like he just invented the lightbulb.

TICKLING! THAT'S IT! It was perfect in many ways: it slowly could drive people crazy, it crawls under their skin, and most importantly, it didn't leave any sort of marks to speak of whatsoever. Forget the intense sexual connotations associated with it – this is exactly how Michael was going to extract the revenge of all revenges. Michael thought for a moment: it's Tuesday now… so perhaps Friday would be the best time to act, to get everything ready. With that firecracker start, Michael knew just one thing and one thing only: he had a lot of work to do before Friday…

The whistle rang out across the gymnasium. Friday's basketball practice had concluded. The guys all made their way to the locker rooms to shower and change. It was an intense practice, and all the guys were pretty exhausted (not having a game for one weekend forced them to really give it their all today). Even as Gene and Michael exchanged a few glares during the game, it was Gene who was surprised by Michael's icebreaker as they began getting into their street clothes.

"Hey Gene", said Michael, clad just in his jeans.

"What?" said Gene, still in the midst of getting his shirt on (his pocketed cargo shorts and flip-flops were already donned).

"I got you something…"

Gene's head cocked sideways. What was this?, he wondered. Gene cautiously walked over to Michael's locker, his leather flips slapping against his meaty size-10 soles. Michael looked around to make sure no one was watching, and pulled a thin brown paper bag from his locker.

"This is for you."

Gene took the parcel, and reached in: it was a very nice bottle of Jack Daniels. Gene quickly looked around to make sure no one was watching as well, then spoke bluntly to Michael:

"Dude, how did you get this?"

"Oh, I got connections man, don't worry."

A bit of a pause as Gene thought for a moment. "Mikey… why exactly did you get this for me?"

Michael then put on the performance of a lifetime: "Well, let's be honest, Gene: there's no love lost between us, especially after gunning for Team Captain like we both did…"

"You got that right," Gene blurted.

"… but anyways, it's been hard for me to admit this, but you really, really have been doing a good job with everything. I know – it sounds kinda weird coming from me, but well, I just think you're leading us in the right direction and… this is my way of saying thank you."

Gene stared at Michael somewhat bewildered… was this really happening? Did a wuss like Mikey finally understand what he had been doing all along: kicking ass as a way to set the example for everyone else on the team?

"Well, um… thanks man."

"Oh don't worry. You deserve it. Where you off to now?"

Michael was done putting his clothes on at this point.

"Oh, I dunno man. Probably just heading back to my place and chillaxin'."

Michael cringed at the use of the word "chillaxin'", but went on regardless:

"Well, hey, need a ride? I got my dad's truck this week."

Michael looked out the locker room windows: it was a late practice today, and the sun had already set… so why the hell not, right?

"Um, sure man. Mind if I drink this a bit now?" he said, referring to the Jack.

Michael smirked: "I'm surprised you didn't start two minutes ago."

Gene smiled at this, and the boys headed off together.

Michael was driving along as Gene quietly sipped his Jack, still quite unsure what to make of the olive branch he had just received. Both guys lived a bit far away from school, but along the same route – Michael's house was first. Without saying anything, he pulled the car over, unable to help but notice that the Jack was already half-empty.

"Hey dude, mind if I grab something from my room first?"

Gene smirked, somewhat drunk already. "Oh, no prob man."

"Actually…" started Michael, "why don't you come in with me? I got something to show you."

"Oh I dunno dude – I'm feelin' a bit tipsy right now and uh… I can get pretty loud. Wouldn't want to bug your parents."

"Oh they're already gone for the weekend dude, you're fine. C'mon."

Not needing further coaxing, Gene came along. Michael, meanwhile, smiled: the hardest part of his plan was 90% complete… and the rest was just a cakewalk.

He opened the sidedoor leading into the basement, and showed Gene his humble abode. Without even looking, Gene sneered "what a dump", but Michael let it slide. Right as the guys entered, the first thing you tend to see in Michael's basement was his fold-out bed, and – completely unmissible to anyone – there were two large pairs of wooden stocks at the head and foot of the creaky bed. Gene – Jack still in hand – then popped a question:

"What the hell is that, man?"

"Oh," said Michael. "That's a project I'm working on for the Theatre Department's upcoming Renaissance Faire." (this was a lie)

"They like… what are they for?"

"Well… ya know what, let me show you Gene. Lie down on the bed there."

"What?"

"Oh please – you telling me that the Team Captain is scared of a simple pair of stocks?"

Gene took the bait: "Pfft, show me."

Gene slipped off his flips and laid down right in the center of Michael's fold-out bed. He was already drunk enough that he didn't even question for a second why there were two pairs of stocks at both the head and foot of Michael's bed. Michael casually opened up the elaborate wooden foot stocks – which Michael had spent quite a bit of time crafting in the last few days – and said "get in".

Gene, smirking with condescension, inched down and placed his ankles right into the open footholes. Michael closed the stocks around Gene's size 10s, and discreetly put a small padlock on them. He went up to the head of the bed and ordered Gene to put his hands through those holes. Amazingly, Gene did so without hesitation. Michael closed them, locked them, and then marveled at the sight: Gene was completely restrained, pretty drunk, and totally unaware of the next several hours that were in store for him.

"You see" started Michael, pleased with his victory already, "in Medieval times, people used to be put in stocks like this for punishment. Public punishment, actually. Often they would just be foot stocks, but I made hand stocks as well just because, well, the more restraint there is, the more fun it is to torture someone."

Gene coughed: "Since when is torturing fun, man? You like a sadist or something?"

Michael laughed a bit. "No no, Gene. But, well, lots of things can be done with someone in your predicament."

"What do you mean my predicament? Let me out of these things, man."

"I'm sorry Gene… that shit just ain't happening right now."

Gene's eyes widened, filled with drunken rage. As Michael expected, the torrent of hatespeech emerged: "WHAT THE FUCK IS THIS MAN?!?! ARE YOU A FUCKING FAG OR SOMETHING?! THIS SHIT AIN'T COOL!!! I'D FUCKING STRANGLE YOU RIGHT NOW IF I COULD YOU QUEER-ASS HOMO!!" Gene trailed off for a bit, but Michael calmly grabbed a pair of rusty scissors from behind him and held them up right to Gene's face.

"Hey Gene – does this look like I'm fucking around?"

Gene stopped. He stared at the scissors, and realized he could be mutilated in a manner of seconds. He piped down.

"Listen dude, I'm… I'm sorry. I didn't mean any of… oh c'mon! Please don't kill me!"

Michael laughed again. "Oh Gene, I'm not gonna kill you – I'm just going to… prepare you."

Both boys were silent as Michael's scissors… slowly began to cut off Gene's shirt. Completely.

Gene was legitimately scared, and Michael knew this. Once he tossed the shirt scraps on the floor, he shelved the scissors, pulled up a chair, and sat right in front of the foot stocks. Gene's size 10 clodhoppers were right there in front of him, completely bound (and what drunken Gene didn't see was that each pair of stocks had been drilled into the basement floor for added security). Michael simply stated "let's have some fun, shall we?" And the evening began…

––––––––––

It started off simply: Michael placed his hands on Gene's feet. He left them there for about five minutes. As soon as his hands touched, he could feel Gene's feet flex and tense up, but after a few minutes – when he realized the hands weren't there to hurt him – they relaxed a bit. Once Michael saw this, he began rubbing Gene's feet, deeply and pleasurably. Gene began lightening up a bit himself: "Dude, if you wanted to give me a foot massage, man, you could've just asked. Seriously. Why don't you let me out of here and we call it a day?" Michael remained silent.

After about 10 minutes, both feet were relatively relaxed, as was the rest of Gene's now-barechested body. Then, Michael took his index finger and softly drug it across Gene's left sole. Gene giggled a bit. "Hey dude, I'm ticklish!" Michael smirked: "I know."

Another fingernail was dragged over the right sole, and Gene laughed again. Then the tickling began. Gene, unsure of what was going on at first, was soon laughing pretty hard. Those firm fingernails of Michael were exploring the contours of Gene's bared foot. The arches. The toes. The ankles. The tops. Michael, in all honesty, didn't completely know what he was doing, but he seemed to enjoy this exploration.

This discovery of Gene's feet. He liked having those two appendages just right there in front of him, wiggling and helpless. Though Gene tried pointing his feet off to the side, Michael's fingernails were just everywhere, digging into his soles one second and fondling his toehairs the next. Michael was actually… kind of enjoying this. Gene was laughing, and thrashing whatever muscles he could: "Dude! STOP! THIS FUCKING TICKLES! HA HA GOD I'MAHA GONNA KILL YOU!" All those threats fell on deaf ears. Michael kept it up, tickling and tickling the bare feet of his enemy – and he was entranced.

All Michael had to do was just move his fingernails up and down Gene's too-soft soles, and the guy's entire body would contort and expend energy at an alarming rate. By doing nothing more than wiggling his fingers, Michael was making Gene smile – completely against his will. Michael had found the human body's trip wire, and he was fully exploiting it: taking his enemy's feet away from him and using them to force emotions into his opponent's body. It was hot. There were moments when a wave of lust took over Michael's body and he just tickled feverishly for about 10-15 seconds, really "getting into it". He looked up every once in awhile, and saw Gene's face go through gruesome distortions, fighting off the smiles and laughter as hard as he could but ultimately to no avail. The body's nervous system was just too much for Gene's high school constitution. Michael, in short, was winning.

Michael stopped after about an hour, and walked up the middle of the bed, and sat down, right next to Gene's extended, immobile arms. Gene was trying to grasp some air, but the hatred inside of him lingered:

"DUDE! WHAT THE FUCK IS THIS?!"

"You have to ask, Gene? C'mon, this is easy: this is revenge."

"What?! What the fuck are you talking about?"

"Revenge for being a dick, Gene. For elbowing me in the face and not apologizing. For ganging up on girls who shun your friends advances for no goddamn reason. For fucking up our team with your arrogance."

Gene, suddenly, seemed a bit hurt. "But… you said I was doing a good job."

Michael was taken back a bit. "Dude... I was lying."

Gene got furious again: "You fucking pansy!! You're dumb as shit, you know that?"

Michael laughed. "Me? No no no, Gene. You're the dumb one. You're the one who, after all, just put your legs in my stocks without any hesitation. Who accepted a gift from your enemy without second-guessing. Who is, shall we say, very 'tied up' at the moment."

"Man, you got to be queer if all you want to do is tie me up and tickle me."

"Really, Gene? That's your comeback? I gotta admit though: tickling you is fun. I really like the idea of having a big, tough guy like you reduced to whimpering jelly just by me wiggling my fingers at your bare feet, man. You see, it's not about the tickling: it's about the helplessness. I put a signal into your body, and you can't even ignore it if you want to. That's why your arms are up in the air right now, Gene, because even if you could move them a BIT, you'd feel more in control now than you're going to feel in a few seconds… where you really, really, really will wish that you could move your arms just an inch."

"Why you say that, Mikey?"

Michael smirked. A single index finger began wiggling at him. Gene's face was filled with terror. It inched slowly – oh so slowly – to Gene's somewhat-hairy armpit. Too slowly. As it got closer, Gene tried twisting his body to avoid it, but it was impossible. He was restrained too tightly. He gripped his lip with his teeth so hard he thought he'd break the skin – but he couldn't do anything. A fingernail began twirling around in his armpit hair, and girlish little giggles and snickers slowly escaped Gene's clenched mouth. Then, without even knowing it, Michael's arm reached around and another fingernail began twirling in his other armpit. Gene was going through sensory overload, and tried so damn hard to keep it under wraps. The fingernails kept slowly twirling and twirling, showing absolutely no sign of mercy whatsoever, the tickle signals wearing down Gene's resistance more and more and more. Sweat formed on his brow as he tried to keep from laughing… but then he broke.

Like a dam busting down, a torrent of uncontrollable laughter flowed from Gene's mouth. It was truly uncontrollable: it's almost as if his voice couldn't keep up with the signals. Even as he practically seizured with smiles, those fingernails kept twirling, mercilessly, watching his victim suffer. Michael was loving it, and began adding onto the psychological torment: "Oh yes, Gene: laugh for me. Laugh like a good little ticklish tickle toy that you are. Say 'I'm your Tickle Toy, Michael!'"

"NEVER!!" Gene shouted before devolving into laughter again.

"Say, 'I'm your Tickle Toy, Michael!'"

"P-p-p-please man! Please stop tickling me!"

"Say, 'I'm your Tickle Toy, Michael!'"

The laughter spewed forth. Gene finally caved "FUCKING HELL I'M YOUR GODDAMN TICKLE TOY, MICHAEL!"

The fingernails kept twirling in those ticklish pits of Gene's.

Michael intoned simply: "Say it again."

"NOOOOOOOOOOO!"

More twirling, swirling tickles.

"Say it again."

"I'm your tickle toy, Michael!"

"Say it again."

"Fuck man!"

"Say it again."

"I'm your tickle toy, Michael! Jesus haha ha!"

"And what do tickle toys do?"

"They… what?"

"Answer me: what do tickle toys do?"

"They… get tickled?"

"I don't mind if I do…"

"FUCCCCCCCCCCCCKKKKKKKKK!"

Hours passed.

Gene's feet were now covered in baby oil, much as how the rest of Gene's body was positively caked in sweat. The fingernails just slid up and down the oiled soles, and Gene – exhausted beyond all belief – kept laughing, albeit 1000x weaker than before. He just existed to be tickled. Gene's fevered brain had been filled with so much tickling it couldn't do much of anything else but just recover. The fingernails on the soles kept dancing, and Gene kept laughing. He had orally agreed to become Michael's lifetime tickle toy about two dozen times already… and Michael loved it each and every time.

Michael's oiled-up hands finally let up. It was god-knows-what-hour. Michael didn't care. As far as he was concerned, he was just getting warmed up. He got some paper towels and wiped his hands clean. He then approached Gene's midsection again.

"Hey Gene."

Ever so faintly: "what?"

"You know what I'm in the mood for?"

"What?"

"Some more armpit tickling. I think there may have been some spots that I missed…"

Michael's hands made a sort of quick grabbing gesture, and soon they descended…

"No no no no noooooooooooooooo!" shouted Gene… before breaking down into tears.

Michael stopped. Gene began genuinely crying out of desperation. "Please, Mikey – I can't take it anymore! I can't… I can't take anymore tickling! I'm so fucking ticklish. Please – I'll do whatever you want. I will literally do whatever the hell you want as long as you promise to stop tickling me."

Michael contemplated this for a second.

"Anything, ay?"

"Yes, anything."

The fingernails abruptly entered Gene's armpits and began dancing. Gene's body shivered and trembled and laughter cackled out of Gene's worn-down vocal chords. Michael continued:

"Like what?"

"I don't know!!! HA HA HA HA you name it!"

"I could use some suggestions, tickle toy…"

"I'll give you my car! I'll give you the ball anytime you want! I… I dunno ha ha ha god I'll suck on your toes Christ!"

Michael stopped.

"You'll what?"

Gene calmed down between bucket breaths.

"I'll suck… suck on your toes if that's what you want. I don't know man."

Michael immediately ripped off his socks and swung his bare feet over to Gene's face. Without any hesitation, Michael just said "Go."

Gene's dry, desperate mouth waited for approximately one nano second before it latched onto the big toe of Michael's left foot. Gene was offering to humiliate himself now, and Michael – whose soft, long toes were being pleasured by a very, very warm mouth – was loving this even more. As Gene systematically went through each of Michael's toes and pleasured them, Michael's index finger slowly circled Gene's navel, just to keep him on task. After a bit, the tears came again. Michael removed his feet and laid down next to his victim.

"What's wrong, tickle toy?"

"Mikey… I'm so tired. I'm just so… I'm so fucking ticklish. I'll never be mean to you again. I swear. I'm a changed man. Please, please, please let me go."

Michael was silent for a moment, and then thought of one last punishment before he let the miserable sap go.

"You've endured quite a lot, Gene. I'll give you that. Personally, I loved every goddamn second of it. I don't mind even telling you that I got a bit of a hardon right now. You're damn right you'll be nicer from now on, because if you aren't, I am going to tickle you even worse than now. But… before I let you go… you have to do me one thing."

"What's that?"

"You have to acknowledge the fact that I'm better than you for the rest of your goddamn life, my ticklish friend."

"OK. How does that work?"

Michael, barefoot, horny, and so pleased with his work he couldn't even describe it, stood up and said just one thing to his fear-stricken, sweat-covered, now-eternally-loyal friend:

"I want you to call me… The Master."

THE CHIP

When I wrote the cathartic, personal "My Ticklish Revenge", I had written it just for me. Although I did post it online, I was somewhat surprised by the reaction I got – several people seemed to enjoy the darker tones of my stories come to the forefront, so I used that encouragement to jump right into this one, a story with an ending that surprised/delighted/terrified even me. This was a long-running fantasy for me, and, well, it still kind of is...

TWO WEEKS PRIOR

Every sexual desire in James' life sat there before him. His devilish little fetishes were going to be satisfied in ways that he never thought possible, and the orgasms that he was going to experience were going to be infinite in number. Heaven was staring at him, and heaven could fit in the palm of his hand.

You see, James was staring at the WaveClick. It was a small microchip that was being developed by TR-Corp, an advanced electronics firm with several military contracts. How did James get to be so lucky as to be standing here at the TR-Corp offices? Simple: he was an intern. James was in the middle of pursuing his Computer Science degree at the local community college, and figured that an internship would be just the thing to put him over the top when evaluation time came. He had been interning (unpaid, natch) at TR-Corp for over a year now, and – aside from being a mere coffee and donut gopher for some of the scientists – had actually endeared himself to several of the senior members of the TR-Corp development team. When he began exhibiting a knowledge of electronics well beyond that of the usual collegiate individual, one TR-Corp staffer forced James to sign a Confidentiality waiver before showing him some of the "Top Secret" things that TR-Corp was working on. WaveClick was one of those things, and it was genius.

Essentially, WaveClick was a small microchip that – when placed at the base of the skull – would modify the brainwaves of an enemy. Literally modify their brainwaves. The chip would come pre-programmed, so that when they were attached to base of an enemy soldier's skull, said soldier could possibly become an instant pacifist, or become suicidal, or homicidal against his own people, or get turned on by near-death experiences, or whatever the chip programmer wanted. By altering brainwaves – and not direct thoughts – one could change someone else's attitude, but not their every movement a la movie hypnotism. WaveClick was essentially a personality modifier, and James, quite frankly, loved the idea of it.

Scientists had already shown him how it works and how it could be programmed, taking time out of the day to show James the complex neural networks that were involved in making a device like that even remotely possible. James ate up every word, line of code, and demonstration that was every conveyed to him about WaveClick, and he was at a point where he could very well program a WaveClick for himself…

… and now, one was left on a desk. Accidentally. Well, of course it was accidentally – each WaveClick prototype was worth about $2 million at this point, and they were always locked up in a super high-security area. Yet here James was – cleaning up after hours at TR-Corp (he was granted a small security clearance to do such a thing), and a scientist had misplaced a $2M WaveClick. James looked around the tidy, too-white walls. No one. It was 9PM, and there was no one around. Having already dusted the security room several times over, James already knew where the cameras were pointing on every floor, and how to sneak his way out of the building undetected… and then proceeded to do so. As far as James was concerned, a scientist was going to lose his job for negligence, the military contractors were going to go apeshit over a lost prototype, the building would go under lockdown, and the community college would soon let him know that his internship would be "indefinitely suspended" until this security issue was resolved. It was almost as if fate had decided to walk right up to the brash young James and simply give him the power of God.

So, late at night, in his one-bedroom apartment, James thought about what the hell to do with a WaveClick now that he had one. Make his teacher give him a good grade? Too easy (and silly, especially for something worth $2M!). Make the president legalize weed? As if he could even get that close! Then, it struck him…

… although James had somewhat of a dominant personality in life, he was somewhat submissive sexually. He didn't like the idea of being dominated as much as he did being used – and this had lead to him fetishizing some… well, some not very common things. Ultimately, when it came to be dominated, he liked the idea of being dominated by a guy more than a girl, and, most interestingly of all, he kind of liked being humiliated by a guy. This (to make a long story short) lead to James having a bit of a foot fetish. He liked the idea of literally (and figuratively) being under a guy, being told to lick a guy's bare sole. To suck the spaces between a guy's toes. To, in essence, being a foot-bitch. Yet that alone wasn't enough for James. He also liked being tickled as well - and though there were more than enough sites to rile up his tickle fantasies, James still hadn't fully explored this particular obsession. He had known – just from the videos he had pursued, that he liked a strong, muscled guy being tied up and literally broken down with the very concept of tickling. Of having wiggling fingers in one's armpits being the ultimate downfall of the indefatigable male ego. A guy getting turned on and jacked off by the mere act of tickling… it was… pretty hot. James, more than anything, would like that done to him.

Yet James' fantasies didn't stop there. There were several guys in his class that he frequently thought about torturing himself. The most frequent one was a friend (well, somewhat of an ex-friend) named Ash. Ash wound up screwing James over on a money deal not too long ago, and it somewhat cooled the best-buddy bond they had shared through the first year and a half of community college. Ash had a bit of a beard, a bit of a Scottish heritage (hence the weekly drink-a-thons), and a perchance for blue jeans and a worn Yankees cap he has. He was blond, a bit hairy, and was the single most frequent jackoff fantasy that James had. The most recent fantasy that teased and delighted James was the idea of Ash being in blue jeans but barefoot and barechested, a blindfold placed securely over his eyes, and having that young boy's body being tied up in a reverse-Y pattern: his legs spread far apart and his wrists bound tightly together, but those arms being stretched out over his head to the max. With Ash still trying to keep both feet planted, he'd be in a state of perpetual tension, to which James would sneak up behind his barechested, confused, and frightened friend, and those fingernails on him would start lightly teasing that armpit hair… and, well, the rest just got James too hard to even think about it.

Oh sure, James would give up just about anything to tickle Ash or – conversely – be dominated by him, but there were others in his class he wanted to do the same to. There was the muscular Jason, the nebbish country-bumpkin Lee, the burlier Gene – really, just the idea of being dominated by close friends of his was enough for James to explode on the inside. Yet it was Ash who had hurt him the most… and it was Ash who would therefore have to pay.

Using a makeshift program that James had been working on for months, James began programming the WaveClick specifically for Ash. He was going to give Ash a few fun personality traits. First off would be a male foot fetish – just like James' own. Ash gave it a two-week delay: it'd start simple enough, but by the end, the only way that Ash would be able to ejaculate would be if the soles of his feet were licked… by a guy. Secondly, James was going to give Ash a bit more of a dominant personality… and to wrap it all off, he'd give Ash a male tickle fetish with a repeater loop: for every time he tickled a guy, his obsession with the tickling would grow more. James didn't even set a limit to it: he just wanted to see how far Ash's fetish would go. Heh, this was going to be fun…

The next day, James was sitting in his Biology class – one that just so happened to be attended by Ash, Gene, Lee, and Jason – his ultimate tickle fantasies. To put his theory to the test, James decided to wear his leather flip-flops in his blue jeans today – his all-time, unabashed favorite look. He was in class a bit early, and a bit nervous – he did, after all, have a $2 million microchip in his hands that he couldn't lose. Students began filing in, and Ash – donning that same NY cap as he did every day – strolled on in, sat down at his desk, and pulled some homework out of his backpack. James made a bold move and decided to sit right next to Ash. They were still kind of friends, so it wasn't an out there move – just an unexpected one. Ash looked up, a bit surprised.

"Oh, hey James."

"Whaddup, Asher Roth?"

"Stop calling me that!"

"But it's fun – you being white and untalented at rapping and all."

Ash smirked a bit.

"Well, James and the Giant Peach,…"

"– hey! –"

"I'm a bit screwed, to be honest. Drank a bit last night, had the assignment half-finished, and forgot the lesson plan by breakfast. So, yeah, just a bit screwed as per usual."

"Well, it happens, don't it? Chin up, ol' pal…"

As James said this last statement, he slapped the back of Ash's neck. A bit hard, but not too much.

"Hey! What's that for?" asked Ash.

"You sober yet?"

"I am now, geez…"

With this, Ash began rubbing his impact zone… but his fingers did not happen upon the newly-implanted WaveClick at the base of his skull – it was small enough to not even feel. James smiled.

The students had assembled, and the teacher was now knee-deep in a discussion about the endoplastic reticulum – riveting, I know. Even though James was copying down notes – pretty much on auto-pilot at this point – all James could think about was what kind of effect this WaveClick was having on his mind. He decided to put this notion to a test. Sneakily, he pulled his iPhone out of his pocket, and got the camera loaded up. Noting that Ash was intently copying down notes, James made a move: he "accidentally" brushed his pen onto the ground. He brushed in Ash's direction, specifically making it out his reach. He whispered to Ash: "Hey, dude, I dropped my pen. Can you grab it for me?" "Oh sure" was the response.

Ash bent down under the desk to grab the pen… oblivious to the iPhone camcorder function that James was training on him. Five seconds later, Ash handed him back his pen, and the lesson continued as normal.

Once James got back into the "flow" of note-taking, he kind of forgot about his person-dominated scheme, and got focused on homework and assignments. Later that night, in his apartment, James was pouring over his notebook – while unshod, naturally – when he totally remembered the iPhone video from earlier. He loaded it up – and, well, the camera angles weren't great. But then… just in the corner of the screen, he could see Ash's face look… at James' own feet. Just briefly, fleetingly, but there was no mistaking what direction those eyes were pointing… and, to top it off, Ash actually moistened his lips! Holy crap! It was working already! James was already getting pretty excited about that, and not too long after, jerked off a big one before slipping into a deep slumber…

ONE WEEK PRIOR

As the week had progressed, James was setting these "little traps" to catch Ash in. They worked each and every time, one video even revealing what could quite possibly be the sight of Ash hiding an erection. One day, after finishing a riveting (cough) discussion on RNA, James began mingling with friends after class. He chatted briefly with Jason (his friend of Italian heritage who just happened to be wearing running shoes and no-show socks today – damn), before he felt a small nest of fingers digging into his soft sides. James naturally recoiled, his body arching to try and avoid the monstrous shock that just forced him to emit a surprised laugh. He turned around and saw Ash – still wearing that damn cap – just staring at him.

"Hey, what the hell was that for?"

"Heh, just checking…" said Ash, somewhat cryptically, before walking away.

James couldn't help but be insanely turned on by that brief little interaction. Could the WaveClick really be working that well? Could Ash suddenly be craving… some tickle torture on James' thin, tickle-prone body? As the week bore on, James' fantasies increased – as did Ash's tickle attacks. Every time, Ash attacked with more relish than before, continually one-upping himself in terms of how much tickle could be distributed to James in a classroom setting without drawing too many glares. James was soon turned on while walking to class, because the thought of being at Ash's fingers just teased and excited him so. Yet, the thing is, James honestly didn't know how this was going to end up – he really didn't know what the WaveClick was actively doing to Ash, which excited him and – quite frankly – terrified him a bit. In truth, it was kind of nice having a bit of physical interaction with the guy he once called his best friend, but the fact that said interaction involved tickling… well, that was just like having his birthday and Christmas rolled into one.

Then next Tuesday rolled around, and soon it was…

DAY ONE

James' bio class was at 1PM, and he usually got up around 10PM in order to eat breakfast and get ready for a trip to the community college and then TR-Corp straight after (although, due to certain lockdowns, it was just his class today). He was surprised, however, to get a knock on his apartment door. Groggy, he looked at his phone and realized it was 9:08AM. Who the hell could be wanting something at this hour? Was it a special delivery from the postman? Did the postman even arrive this early? James – dressed in a white t-shirt and some pajama pants, groggily made it to the door. The knocking continued. "I'm coming! I'm coming!" he shouted. He opened the door only to see…

… Ash. Standing there. Looking quite chipper given the hour even. James was a bit taken back, and surprised even.

"Um…. hey there, Ash."

"Hiya."

"Um… what's up?"

"May I come in?"

"Yeah, sure. I guess."

James opened up the door and let Ash in – wearing a leather jacket, what appeared to be a vintage rock T-shirt underneath, some dark blue jeans, and his usual shin-high white socks and some solid black sneakers (and that damn Yankees hat, of course). Ash invited himself in, and James closed the door behind him. Ash took the unusual step of turning around and locking James' door behind him. James, still groggy and very confused, wasn't quite sure what to say.

"So, um… what's going on, Ash? Is everything OK?"

Ash, calmly, removed his leather jacket and hung it up on the hook next to James' door. He did the same with his hat. It's at this moment that James noticed that Ash had a small travel bag with him, which was placed gently on the ground. That lightly bearded boy then stood up, turned to Ash, and smiled a devious grin. He took a small step towards James, and then another – still silent. James instinctively backed up one… and then the hands reached out. James turned to run but it was too late – Ash had grabbed him in a bear hug and soon brought James to the ground. All Ash whispered was one very simple sentence: "Ticklish much?"

James screamed a bit – but he was on the ground and Ash was on top of him, weighing his body down. Ash's fingers then crawled and danced over James ticklish ribcage, and the laughter ensued. Those little fingers were digging into all of James' worst spots, and James was so confused, all he could do was laugh. Little cackles teased and edged out of him, Ash's body weighing down on and squeezing the deep-seated laughs out of James like rolling through a tube of toothpaste. Ash's favorite thing was to take his index fingers and jab them right into James' armpits and wiggle them around. Just the index fingers – like two devious little tickle sticks shoved right into James' ground zero. Of course, James' armpits were hairy, and each small rotation of those fingers just moved and twirled those little hairs around in there, giving Ash those all-important Bonus Tickles that were great in driving someone insane. James, awake for only four minutes now, was in Tickle Hell.

Although James tried fighting off Ash's hands, there was something different about his friend this day: he was intent on tickling his buddy. He wasn't stopping, and he wasn't taking no for an answer. Any time James tried to hold up a hand to block him, Ash grabbed it and slammed James' wrist down the ground, putting James in an awkward position that – no matter what – at least opened up some new tickle spot on him. It wasn't long before James had flipped over, lying face up and barefoot while Ash pressed his body weight down. Those meaty Ash hands had now began exploring his thighs, and suddenly those squeezes to those hamstrings sent James' voice up an octave. "Puh-pulease!!" was about all James could get out. He couldn't even get out the "Stop!" that would invariably follow. Ash, for whatever reason, was suddenly this world-class tickle freak, and he knew how to diversify, to keep his victim on nervous edge the entire time. If James had any other thought aside from "HOLY FUCK THIS TICKLES LIKE HELL!!!!", it would be that Ash was very, very impressive with his skills.

Those hands on the thighs were feeling James tickle flesh through his pajama pants, and it wasn't long before they made their way to James crotch... and James' hardon. In truth, James hadn't even noticed how hard he was until Ash grabbed his cock through the pants fabric like a joystick. The tickling stopped momentarily. James, still in aftershocks of laughter, looked up at Ash, who got another devious smile. Then the words that followed: "Hmmmm... wonder what we have here?" James immediately went red with embarrassment, and before he could even react, Ash pulled a freaking pair of handcuffs right out of his back jeans pocket... and handcuffed James' hands behind his back. James was stunned, and next thing he knew, his ankles were handcuffed together! Holy shit – this entire thing was premeditated to the T! James looked at the small bag that lay there next to his apartment door… and shuddered to think what else was in there.

Yet James didn't have time for this! As he regained his composure, James was beginning to wrap his head around what had just happened. 30 minutes ago, his friend had burst into his apartment, tickled him into horny submission, and now had him bound very tightly. This… wasn't right. James wanted to protest, but it was at this moment that he realized just how out of breath he was… he couldn't even form a sentence. Ash, meanwhile, had picked up the handcuff chain between his two ankles, and began dragging James across his own apartment and to his own couch. Ash left James at the coffee table in front of the couch. James simply laid there, overwhelmed. He did see, however, from his carpet-level perspective, Ash toe his sneakers off. He caught a glimpse of the soles of Ash's white socks – and they were kind of dirty. Like, Ash had worn them for two straight days kind of dirty. Ash walked over to James' kitchen area and found a bag of pretzels and beer from the fridge. He walked over to the couch, turned on James' TV, and propped his feet up so his feet were just barely hanging over the coffee table. James was still on the floor. An early-morning baseball game was on TV (the Dodgers), and Ash sat there, very content with himself.

After a few minutes of baseball commentary jetted by James' ear, he soon kneeled up – kneeling being the only real position he could make with his hands cuffed behind his back and his feet chained – and was kneeling facing… Ash's socked feet. He had to tone things down a bit, because this was too much.

"Hey Ash…"

"You got a foot fetish, don't ya?" Ash didn't even look at James as he said it.

James had a look of shock creep across his face. He was stunned, blown away by the sheer bluntness of that statement. If there was ever a doubt in James' mind, Ash was now a full-on dom.

"I… well, yes I kinda…"

"My feet turn you on, don't they?"

"I…"

Ash's socked right foot reached out and stroked James' raging erection through his pajama pants. James succumbed to a moment of weakness:

"Fuckin' hell your feet turn me on sir."

The statement tumbled right out of him. Ash turned briefly to James and showed off that trademark shit-eating grin of his.

"Sniff them… but don't get your head in the way of the screen."

Ash looked back at the TV, and James… was still stunned. There was no bullshitting around with Ash now, and he would have to realize that…

"I said sniff them, bitch!"

James went into horny slave autopilot. His nose dove into those socks, landing right at the base of the toes, and inhaled.

Christ, that was amazing. The sweet scent of male foot sweat, flaring up and dancing around his nostrils, each full-bodied inhalation through the nose filling up James' frame with a horniness he had never known before. Had he looked, James would see the precum becoming so prominent that it had actually made a visible stain on the outside of his pajama pants (which were already housing a pair of cotton boxers). For a few minutes, James' brain shut off and his libido took over, each intake of Ash-funk getting him closer and closer to orgasm. His hips began subconsciously thrusting with each and every breath. James may have very well gotten off from the smell alone had Ash not barked another order from his pretzel-filled mouth:

"Take my socks off with your teeth. Slowly. I want to see you enjoy it."

James, again, didn't hesitate. It took a bit for the teeth to really grip the rim of Ash's socks, but once he did, it took a few attempts to slowly drag that rim down his shins, past the heel, over the sole, across the ball, and... revealing the toes. Ash's right foot was now bare, and his toes instinctively flexed a bit as he felt the nice warm air of James' apartment surround them. Without thinking, James placed his nose right at the base of James toes again, and inhaled. FUCK that could've been a cumshot right there. Not getting away from his task too much, James did the same for Ash' left foot, and then sat back, ogling the sight before him: his lust object Ash, eating some pretzels, drinking a beer, in blue jeans, with bare feet sticking out of them right on his very own coffee table. James ultimate fantasy had come true... well, it hadn't fully come true until his newly-minted master said the following: "Now, lick my feet."

Those words danced in his head. "Lick my feet", coming right from Ash's lips. Those three words had echoed in countless masturbatory fantasies for James, and to hear them actually form in front of him... there was no ending to the feeling of elation he felt. Without hesitation, James dug in. His tongue was like an artisans paintbrush, and Ash's soles were the canvas of which to paint his masterpiece. His tongue darted between Ash's hairy toes, licked from heel-to-toe in one motion like a giant paint stroke on a house, and James even lightly chewed the hairs on the tops of Ash's perfect size-10s with relish. James got lost in the motions. After a bit, he began flicking his tongue on the tips of Ash's toes, and then looked up. Ash had unzipped his jeans, pulled his hard cock out, and was jerking with his eyes closed. The more that James licked, the more furious that Ash jerked it – and before long,

Ash's hips arched, James mouth tried to fit as many Ash-toes as it could into it, and Ash let out a streaming cum shot that almost hit the rim of that damn baseball cap. Both 20-somethings sat there, in the elation of it all. Ash was melted to the couch, blissful. He then snuck out one more order to his foot slave:

"Get yourself off before I change my mind."

As if James needed convincing.

The tongue lashed out to his master's soles and began to lick. When he couldn't take it anymore, James asked for a bit of an assist, and Ash's right foot gripped the top of his pajama pants between his big and first toe, and helped pull those pesky pants – and the boxers – down. Then, James lived out his fantasy: Ash's soles still slick from their saliva coating, James rubbed his sensitive tip against his friends soles. Within five seconds he came on them with a fury that he had never known. James, exhausted (and his jaw hurting a bit), then fell back on the floor. He looked up, and could see a faint bit of his own semen on the edge of the table. For some reason, James thought it funny, and then promptly passed out.

When James awoke, his body wouldn't move. James was in his bedroom, and he was tied spread eagle to his small metal-framed bedset. And he was tied spread-eagle tight. He looked at the straps on his ankles and wrists – these were professional-grade bondage straps. In walked Ash, silent and grinning as usual… with a blindfold in his hand. James, weak, stuttered a "no" out of his mouth, but his still-in-jeans friend quietly walked over and covered up James' eyes. All he could do was feel his helpless body now… and feel the reactions it was about to experience. Then…

… nothing happened. For ten minutes. James' muscles were tense with anticipation, knowing very well that a tickle could be coming RIGHT NOW… but nothing. Then, out of nowhere, Ash jumped on the bed, kneeling right in the space where James' forcibly-spread legs were, Ash's knees barely an inch away from James' balls. Instinctively, James tried to squirm, but he was tied fucking tight. His muscles barely moved. Ash then began speaking…

"So, James… tell me about some of your deepest sexual fantasies."

"Wait, what?"

"Tell me whose feet you want to lick and tickle."

"How the fuck do you know all of this, Ash?"

"I know the signs, my friend. I got a bit of a foot fetish myself, and I can tell when someone is looking at my feet. They are sexy, aren't they? Say, 'I get hard when you're barefoot, Master Ash.'"

"Listen, I…"

Before James could do anything, Ash's hands – like military-trained tickled spiders, attacked James' ribcage like they were on a tickle kamikaze mission. Whooping in surprise, James fought and reeled and but couldn't do anything: not having any sort of motion made the tickling that much more intense, and James was pleading in mere seconds.

"Please stop!!!"

"Then say it!"

"I get hard when you're barefoot, Master Ash!"

"Say it again!"

"I GET HARD WHEN YOU'RE BAREFOOT, MASTER ASH!"

Ash was satisfied, but not completely. Ash's fingers began twirling around James' armpits and nipples slowly as Ash gradually extracted all of the sexual fantasies James had ever had. He talked about how he went to see a movie with Lee once and tried to take a picture of his flips-and-jeans feet with his camera phone, and nearly got caught, and how hot that espionage was. He talked about the time he was staying over at Jason's, waited until he was passed out drunk, and sucked on his friends toes until he came, Jason unconscious and oblivious to the entire thing. He spilled the beans on how he kept fantasizing about Gene's clodhoppers ever since he saw them bare for the first time over at a poker night. It was all frightfully embarrassing, but Ash was eating every detail up. Then… James came clean…

… about WaveClick.

Ash stopped. James babbled on about what it did and how this was all great but very intense and if Ash wanted to stop all of this, he could just dig in and remove the small chip on the base of his skull. James said all of this in a way that was almost pleading. Ash sat there and mulled it over…

"But James… I like tickling you."

"Well… well of course you do! You're programmed to think that!"

"But, you don't understand, buddy – I really like tickling you."

"Don't you want to stop that?"

"Tickle tickle…"

"No, Ash, please! Pleashshahahaaha!"

James was then treated to a five-hour non-stop no-holds-barred tickle session. Again, he passed out the second it was over.

DAY TWO

James was about to cum, and he just barely woke up.

It took a second for James to realize, but he had been wrapped in a cocoon made out of his own bedsheets, and those bedsheets where taped around his mummified body pretty damn tightly. What James was surprised about was that his phone had been wedged right into the space between his balls and up against his prostate. The alarm was going off. Apparently, Ash had set James' phone to vibrate. And the alarm was going off. Vibrating right against his manly pleasure arena. BUZZ then stop. BUZZ then stop. The alarm… wasn't stopping. For obvious reasons, James couldn't hit the snooze. He was wrapped up very tightly in his own cum-stained bedsheets, his head sticking out of one end and his bared size 11 feet sticking out the other. As far as James could tell, it was around 6AM. Ash was sleeping on the couch. James couldn't say anything as his voice had gone hoarse. Ash wouldn't wake up for another three hours.

When Ash – just in boxers now – did wake up, he picked up his phone and called James' phone – it buzzed again, but when the call was over, the alarm had stopped. Holy shit, though James, how the fuck did Ash know to do that? Again, the premeditation to this thing was amazing. James went into the kitchen and got out a bowl. He draped his dirty socks at the bottom of it and then poured some cereal over them, filling the bowl. Ash walked over and placed the bowl right at James face. Ash then said "I'm taking a shower. Whatever you don't eat when I get back is thrown out."

Ash began using James' place like his own. Ash ate through the cereal – he desperately needed whatever nutrients could be sucked out of those Captain Crunch doodads – but as he got further down the bowl, the more that Ash-foot smell permeated. Ash had thought this through, and the more that James ate, the hornier he got. In a few minutes time, he was using his tongue to scoop up stray little cereal bits, just as his tongue graced the soles of Ash's socks. What a fucking genius move: start out the slave hungry and have him be rock-hard horny (and distracted) by the end of the meal. As terrified as James was, he couldn't help but be blown away by the evil genius of Ash's plans.

The rest of the day was pretty simple: still cocooned, Ash brought out James' laptop and set it right in front of his face. Ash got to tickle and lick James' feet A LOT, and before long, James had given up every single personal password that he had. After Ash got into James e-mail account and began sending out elaborately-worded e-mails to James' school, parents, and other associates (offering his feet and a lickable incentive for James' silence as Ash wrote), Ash then had James showing him where, exactly, on his computer, James' foot and tickle videos/pics where. Ash put all of the pictures on a slideshow, and then, with James feet in his greedy hands, lightly tickled the slaveboys soles as he asked James for a detailed description on why he downloaded each and every pic and what about it made him horny. It was, again, humiliating as all fuck, and it took six hours. By the time Ash was done, James passed out yet again, and slept through the night and for most of the next day.

DAY FOUR

When James awoke this time, he was blindfolded. Yet he was strung up differently. He was standing, but his arms were pulled WAY over his head and tightly together. His legs were far apart and… oh no! That position! That position that James always wanted to see Ash in – he was now in it! And very naked. And very ticklish. The very fact that James was in this position gave him a very nervous kind of hardon, but that faded when he realized… he wasn't being touched.

An hour passed. Then two. Then three.

Then, his hearing now the only real sense he had going for him being immobile and blindfolded like this… he heard footsteps near his apartment door. Several footsteps. And some talking. Some excited-sounding talking. The keys went into James' apartment door lock… and then it opened.

"AND HERE HE IS!" shouted Ash.

"Awesome!"

"Cool!'

"He doesn't even fucking know what's going to happen to him!"

Those voices… they… no.

Yes, they were the voices of Lee, Jason, and Gene. Jesus Christ – Ash was bringing them over to show off his handiwork. Wouldn't they be disgusted though? A little scared maybe?

"What the fuck are they doing here, Ash?!"

The next 12 words out of Ash's mouth forever altered James life:

"It's amazing how hard it is to steal a couple of WaveClicks…"

Immediately, James struggled as hard as he could, calling on his last remaining strength to perhaps pull the ropes holding his arms up down from the ceiling (or whatever contraption they were hanging from), trying to uproot his spread legs from the ground… but no. It was pointless. Nebbish little Lee, strong ol' Jason, and burly Gene were surrounding their naked, ticklish prey. Then the fingers descended… oh the fingers.

A few collective cumshots later (and a quick supper), James – now too weak to ever show any kind of resistance – was again tied spread eagle on his bed, but not blindfolded. James was still trying to figure out A> how Ash broke into TR-Corp, B> steal three more WaveClicks, and C> somehow find a way to program each one of them to the exact same settings his was on. The guys had set up four chairs around the bed, and were propping their bare soles right up on the mattress itself – perfectly in James' line of vision. They were eating sandwiches on paper plates, talking about sports teams and hinting at some of the things they were going to do with their tickle toy. Then, the thin and eager Lee tossed out an idea:

"Hey Ashy: didn't you say that James had different fantasies for each of us?"

"Yup."

"Well here's an idea – let's round-robin him. One guy straddles him and tickles his pits while interrogating him about every little detail of that fantasy, two guys lick James' soles, and the other guy uses the video camera to film these things!"

"WHERE THE HELL DID YOU GUYS GET A VIDEO CAMERA FROM?" yelled James, but his screams fell on deaf ears.

"But," started Gene, "when do we stop tickling him? When he's done telling the humiliating fantasy?"

"No, smirked Lee, sporting an evil grin that he was obviously flashing for the first time, "we tickle him until he cums!"

All the guys had an amazing "a-ha" moment at that idea, and James almost burst into tears… at least until Lee's bony fingers dug into his ribs and the rollercoaster began.

Eight hours later, James had his fifth orgasm in a row (the guys discovered that licking James' body produced some really fun reactions) – and it was a total dry-shot. It was simultaneously the most wonderful and horrible thing he had ever felt in his life.

EIGHT MONTHS LATER

The only reason that any of the five tickle freaks left the apartment these days was to get food, and they did it quite begrudgedly: four of them were getting more and more addicted to tickling James, as if there obsession wasn't already deep-rooted enough. Just like Ash, the other three could only cum when their soles were licked, and James' jaw was getting more and more exhausted every day. Money wasn't a problem anymore: TickleJames.com had become an overnight sensation, known for being the single most merciless tickle site to ever hit the web. The guys' favorite part was when the $100-a-month VIP subscribers suggested devious new ideas. A huge hit was the day when the guys took a field trip out the beach. They dug a huge hole in the sand, put James in it, and buried him packed tight so that only his head was sticking out. The guys put up a beach umbrella, put towels all around James head, put their beach chairs facing inwards in a circle around him, and pawed his head with their feet for hours, filming him desperately sucking everyone's toes as they downed more and more beers and got drunker and hornier.

After only eight months, TickleJames.com had proved so popular that the guys were able to buy many wonderful things. New tickle brushes, new bondage sets, and – one fateful day, a black market WaveClick 2.0 – the kind that permanently altered brain waves. James voice had long since gone, so he couldn't scream his objections as the guys gathered around their table – James, as always, tied underneath and servicing feet – and discussed what they wanted in a "perfect slave". James mind was warped now, and he could barely hear those conversations – yet he was none the less terrified the day the held him down on the floor, and proceeded to attach a WaveClick to the base of James' skull. He tried to scream, but then the WaveClick was snapped into place...

...and then the real fun began.

HOW TO BE A TICKLE SLAVE

(In 10 Easy Steps)

1. **Be ticklish.**

   It may seem simple, but the best way to serve a Tickle Master is to be tickled early and often, so you know just *how* ticklish you are. Know what spots are the worst, which ones drive you the most insane, and what tickle tools work best on you. This knowledge will be invaluable later on.

2. **Do what is asked of you.**

   If your Master has ordered you to remove your shoes upon entering his lair, then dammit you better remove your shoes. A good Slave knows that every word that comes out of his Master's mouth is gospel, and it shouldn't be messed with. Yet even with that said…

3. **Break at least ONE rule.**

   It may seem odd, but you should break at least one of your Master's rules early on. Why? So you know just what kind of punishment you're in for. You are designed to be tickled, after all, and by showing just the faintest hint of disobedience early on, it will only egg your Master on to unleash an even more brutal punishment than originally planned.

4. Exert stamina.

A good Slave won't complain about being tied in the same position for five hours at a time. A good Slave will ask for a bathroom break prior to tickling so that he doesn't have to interrupt a particularly delicious tickle session. A good Slave will *work* to become a good Slave – it's not just something that happens overnight.

5. Ask to be tied tighter.

Everyone knows that the best kind of tickle victims are the ones that are helpless. If there's even a *little* bit of wiggle room in your restraints, a good Slave will ask his Master to tie them tighter, so that the faintest hint of escaping his deserved torture is removed from the equation altogether.

6. Learn how to beg.

Unless gagged by your Master, a good Tickle Slave will know when to beg for more. Even as you can't stand it, even as your mind gets warped and distorted into unrecognizable shapes, a good Slave will ask for more tickling against their better judgment. It will, after all, make your Master very happy…

7. Learn how to properly worship.

Tickle and foot fetishes are often (but not always) interconnected, and a Tickle Slave that's worth his weight will know how to do proper foot service, using their tongue to lap up the taste of his Master's soles and the smell of his discarded socks. A good Slave will learn to appreciate every flavor that emanates from his Master, and that shall be the Slave's sustenance.

8. Be an open book.

A good Slave will let his Master know his every fantasy, no matter how humiliating or embarrassing it may be. A good Slave will not question a tickle-laced interrogation, or whether or not it's recorded. A good Slave is the property of his Master, and a good Slave should act as such.

9. Learn everything there is to know about your fetish.

A good Slave shouldn't just stop at his Master's recommendations. A good Slave – at the appropriate time – should recommend even better bondage positions, tickle tools to use, and situations to be placed in. A good Slave researches his surroundings, his desires, and his limits, and shall ask his Master to break all his expectations should he so desire.

10. Love your ticklishness.

The only reason books like this get made is because millions of guys share the same addiction: of tickling and of being tickled. A good Slave is comfortable with this, fully aware of just how horny the very thought of tickling makes him and how horny it should make his Master. Slaves come and go, but a great Slave is the kind that wants more, and loves to be tickled, that wants their limits warped and shattered. A few Slaves even break out T-shirts that say "TICKLISH" across the front in big bold letters, advertising their weakness/desires to the entire world. A great Slave is unafraid of his fetish, and an even greater Slave notes if he finds the initial inklings of said fetish in others. Perhaps there's a great Master lurking in your closest friend… And perhaps it will take a great Slave to bring that quality out in them…

ABOUT THE AUTHOR

James T. Medak is a pseudonym for a writer whose of love of tickling and foot worship has gone on for years. He's had dozens of encounters and is constantly seeking hundreds more. He currently resides in the great (and utterly strange) state of Utah.

www.ingramcontent.com/pod-product-compliance
Lightning Source LLC
Chambersburg PA
CBHW050658290626
47170CB00015B/1643